AN ENTANGLED CHRISTMAS

A MERGE SERIES CHRISTMAS NOVEL

KYLIE KENT

MCCARTNEY INDUSTRIES PTY LTD

AN ENTANGLED CHRISTMAS
A MERGE SERIES CHRISTMAS NOVEL

Kylie Kent

Social Media:
Website & Newsletter: www.kyliekent.com
Facebook: @kyliekent2020
Instagram Follow: @author_kylie_kent_

This book contains scenes of sexual acts, profanity, and violence. If any of these are triggers for you, you should consider skipping this read.

To Nana, you are the one who instilled a love for all things Christmas. You gave me the best Christmas memories I have as a child. Thank you for being you!

THE MERGE FAMILY

Who is who in the merge family? This world all begun with Zac & Alyssa and grew into more than I ever could have imagined it to be.

Below is the family tree's of all the characters you'll read about in both The Merge Series.

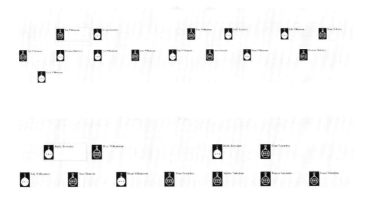

The Merge Family

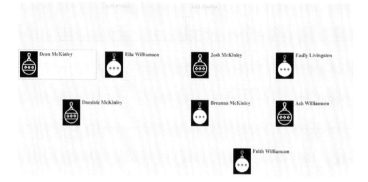

PROLOGUE

Alex

"*I* don't care what it costs. I want that fucking house! Make it happen, or I'll find an agent who can do their fucking job." I disconnect the call and slam the phone down on the desk.

I've been trying to secure the deal on this house for two weeks now. It's October, and I want that house settled by Christmas. My niece wants a beach Christmas, and I plan on giving her one. The fact that this beach property happens to be right next door to the McKinleys is a bonus.

I've been working on a multimillion-dollar merger with McKinley Industries for months now. The owner's hesitant to get into business with me. I need to show him that I'm a family man, just like he is. Besides, I've heard the rumours about Joshua McKinley—his past ain't all rainbows and sunshine.

He's a full-blooded psychopath in an Armani suit. Blood stains designer labels the same way it darkens the second-hand clothing I grew up with. The only difference between Joshua McKinley and me is he was born into that world. Me? I built my empire from the ground up. My wealth has literally come at the cost of the blood, sweat, and tears of my enemies.

Anyone who's dared to cross me, undermine me in either my legitimate businesses or my alternative ventures, found out very quickly exactly who they were dealing with. Not many of them lived to tell the tale. The few who have survived my wrath, only did so as a strategic move on my part.

If you don't have anyone to tell the stories, to spread the rumours, then how the hell are people meant to get the warning? The one that says not to fuck with me, or what's mine. I suppose the few strung-up bodies and posted-out digits would have sufficed. While such acts could never be traced back to me, there was no doubt who was responsible. Not from anyone in the Sydney region.

People whispered my name, in fear that saying it too loudly would somehow make me appear. *People are fucking idiots.* Especially the real estate agent who is failing to secure this fucking property for me.

"Do you really need to yell, Alessandro? Tessie is sleeping. If you wake her, you're dealing with her for the night. *Not me.*" My sister Mia stomps her foot, probably louder than I was speaking just now.

"That's not really a threat. You know I'd stay up with her all night if I needed to." I can never say no to my niece. Apart from my sister, she is my biggest weakness. One I'll pay any price to protect.

"That's not the issue. She needs to stay in routine. What's going to happen when she starts school next year? She can't be having all-nighters with her crazy uncle, then go to school the next day. She's five, Alex, not twenty-five."

"I'm aware of how old she is, Mia. And as for school, we will cross that bridge when we get to it. Besides, I don't see why she has to go to school when there are perfectly good teachers I can hire to tutor her. It'd probably cost half as much as the fees at the school anyway."

"She's not being homeschooled, Alex. She needs to socialise, to make friends who are not old men working for her uncle."

"Argh, I'm not fucking old! Not even fucking close. I can give you a demonstration of just how not fucking old I am *if you'd like*." That comes from Leo, my second

3

in command, and my fucking about-to-be-ex best friend *if he keeps hitting on my sister*.

Picking up the letter opener from my desk, I fling it across the room. It embeds in the wall a hair to his left. "Next time, that will be directed at a fucking eye. Stop hitting on my sister."

"It's not my fault your sister is hot." He laughs as he ducks the paperweight that flies at his head.

"Stop! You don't have to worry, Alex. I wouldn't sleep with Leo if he were the last man on earth," Mia yells as she storms out the door.

"I've heard that speech before, Mia!" I yell back. I stop myself from adding the "and where did that get you" part of the sentence. As fucking furious as I was at the time, I wouldn't change a thing now. Because that mistake of Mia's gave us Tessie. And nothing about that little girl is a mistake, apart from her waste-of-space sperm donor, who no longer resides on this fucking planet.

The ringtone of my phone deafens me. It's my real estate agent—*again.*

"You better have good news for me," I answer.

"It's done—4.2 mil. Settles in four weeks. The house will be yours just before December. Congratulations, Alessandro."

"Perfect. Send my assistant the documents."

"It was a pleasure doing business with you, sir."

"Wish I could say the same." I hang up. I don't

waste time with small talk. Time is money, and my time is something that guy cannot bloody afford.

I smile at Leo. "Looks like it's going to be a beach Christmas."

He groans. I know he hates the beach. It's like the guy was born to be a vampire, never wanting to go anywhere hot or sunny. Why the fuck he chooses to live in Sydney is beyond me. It's hot and sunny here more often than not.

"Really, why? All that sand, sun... it's overrated. Why don't we fly to Canada? Have ourselves a white Christmas?" he grunts.

"Tessie wants Christmas at the beach." I shrug.

"So you bought a whole house? Have you never heard of Airbnb?"

"I like the house. *I like the neighbours even more.* Stop complaining and start making the arrangements to install as much security as possible. It has to be discrete; we need to blend in out there."

"You don't blend in anywhere, Alex," he says as he walks out the door.

1

Lily

I pull up behind my parents' car; they know I'm here. You can't *not* hear my Monaro purr as she drives up. Do they stop the disgusting level of PDA they currently have going on? *No.* I slam my door to get their attention, then silently apologize to the car. It's not her fault my parents are so bloody gross.

"Eww, Dad, just stop. People can see you. The neighbours don't want to be blind for Christmas."

My dad stops giving my mum mouth-to-mouth in the driveway. "Lily, sweetheart, glad you made it here in one piece. And trust me, anyone who gets a glimpse of your mother is a lucky son of a bitch."

"Thanks, and still *eww*. For the love of God, tone it down a bit. That's what bedrooms were made for, you know."

Dad tilts his head at me. My father, *the* Bray Williamson. Nothing ever gets past him when it comes to me or my twin sister, Hope. "Lily, you don't know what happens in a bedroom, other than you go there to sleep. *Right*?" he asks.

I'm sure he knows I'm not a virgin. I'm twenty-five for crying out loud. Since he's determined to gross me out, payback is going to be a bitch for him right now. Smiling sweetly, I say, "Daddy, I'm twenty-five and my entrance into the nunhood flew out the window a long, long time ago." I leave him there for my mum to deal with.

"Take that back, Lily Hope Williamson. That is not true," he yells after me.

"Bray, calm down. She's an adult. Stop acting like you don't know." I hear my mum trying to talk sense into him.

Walking into the house, I go in search of my Aunt Ella. This is her beach-front property. Her husband, my Uncle Dean, bought it for her as a gift when they first got together. We've spent many Christmases here. As the years have gone by, it's squishier than it used to be, but I wouldn't have it any other way. I love my family, and Christmas is my absolute favourite holiday.

"Ah, hi," I call out as I enter the kitchen, where my Aunt Ella is lecturing my Aunt Lyssa on why you can't use so much flour. Both of my aunts are currently covered in the clumpy white powder. The usually pristine white marble kitchen is a disaster zone.

"Oh, Lily Pilly, thank goodness you're here. Honey, do me a favour and get Aunty Lyssa out of my kitchen before I kill her, and then Uncle Zac kills me, then Uncle Dean kills him—the killing spree won't end until we're all dead, really," Aunt Ella huffs, before adding, "Actually, Josh and Emily will be the only ones to survive. No one's crazy enough to take on Emily."

"Wow, sounds like you've put a lot of thought into this." I laugh.

"You have no idea the shit I have had to deal with over the years." She starts pushing Aunty Lyssa out of the kitchen.

"Wait! I'm getting better. I almost had it this time," Aunt Lyssa says, wiping her hair out of her face.

"Almost had what?" In comes the growly voice of my Uncle Zac. Out of all my uncles, he's by far my favourite. I mean, Uncle Dean's great. And Josh, even though he's not technically my uncle, he still kind of is (my Aunty Ella is married to his brother, my Uncle Dean). And Josh would definitely be the one I'd call to bail me out of anything I didn't want my dad to know about.

But Uncle Zac, he's my number one. "Lil, how are you?" he says as he hugs me tight.

"I'm better, now that you've saved me from these two nuts." I squeeze him back. For a man in his fifties, he's still as fit as a thirty-year-old. He's also vain as hell, and the way into his good graces is to compliment him on his looks.

"Uncle Zac, have you been living at the gym? You're looking mighty fit," I say, punching his stomach.

He pretends that my jab hurts him. I know it doesn't. "Ouch, what's with all the women in this family knowing how to hit better than I do? And you're my favourite, Lil. Why the hell are you hitting me?"

"Aww, well, don't tell Uncle Dean, but you're my favourite too." I wink.

"Remember when I was your favourite?" Aunty Ella pipes up from the sink, where she's started washing dishes.

"Don't worry, El, you're still my favourite sister." Uncle Zac laughs, then turns to Aunt Alyssa. "Sunshine, you look like you could use a shower. I can help you with that."

"Eww, gross. What the hell is wrong with you all? There are children around." I stick my finger in my mouth, in a mock gag.

"Children? Last I looked, they all went and grew up," Aunty Ella comments.

"Well, those grown-up children don't want to see the oldies making out, or hear about their plans to. It's gross."

"*Please,* Lily, it's not like you've never kissed anyone," Aunt Lyssa says. "Besides, when someone like Zac Williamson kisses you, you don't have a care in the world as to who sees it."

"No, she hasn't kissed anyone, sunshine. Lil, boys have cooties. Stay away from them," Uncle Zac grunts out.

"I'm going to tell you what I just told Dad: *my entry into the nunhood sailed away a long time ago.* But that doesn't mean I want to see the PDA between all the oldies. Maybe I'll just bring a boy home and start making out with him in front of everyone."

"You could try, Lily, but he won't last too long before he's fucking pig food." I jump ten feet in the air. Where the hell did he come from?

Turning around, I stare at Josh. "Really, you think I'd let any of you crazy fuckers near a guy I date? Why do you think you've never met any of them? Because you're all nuts—*the lot of you.* You'd scare them away before I even got a goodnight kiss." I throw my hands in the air.

Uncle Josh comes over and hugs me. "Lily, any guy who isn't man enough to stand up to your overprotective family doesn't deserve you anyway. You find someone who will never back down for you," he whispers in my ear.

"Well, if you see him first, be sure to send him my way." I laugh. I need to escape. I've been here all of ten minutes, and I already need a break. I'm used to having Hope or one of my cousins around to share the craziness of our parents, but I'm the first one to arrive.

"Aunt Ella, is it the usual room?" I ask.

"Sure is, sweetheart. You, Hope, and Ava. Then I have Axel and Dominic in the room next to you," Aunt Ella says.

"Where's Ash staying? And where is everyone? Why am I the only one here?" I ask. I'm usually the last to arrive; it's weird being first.

"Ash rented a house just down the street. But he will be spending most of his time here. He just wanted a quiet place to work. Axel and Dominic are already out surfing," Aunt Lyssa explains.

There are seven of us kids. Ash is my Uncle Zac and Aunt Lyssa's first child. He's also the oldest, at twenty-eight. Then they have Ava (she's eighteen) and Axel, who's just turned sixteen. My Aunt Ella and Uncle Dean have one child: Dominic, who is nineteen. Then there's me and my twin sister, Hope. We're twenty-five. Oh, and Breanna, who has just turned twenty-two. She is Josh and Emily's daughter, and also Dominic's cousin, since Uncle Dean and Josh are brothers.

"When's Ava getting here? She's going to be pissed I got the first choice of beds." I laugh. Ava is the most precious of us all, the little princess of the group. You would think it'd be Breanna, considering she's literally the heiress to McKinley Industries. Her name and picture are continually splashed all over the papers for being the wealthiest kid in the country. Yet, Bree is the one who isn't bothered by glitz and glamour.

Don't get me wrong... she's stunningly beautiful, and dresses to kill everywhere she goes. But when she's around just us family, she's usually in yoga pants and a t-shirt, with her hair left undone and no makeup. Unless it's an event where Ash is in attendance, then she goes full-on glam queen.

Bree and Ash have the whole "I want you but I can't have you" thing going on. They both lust after each other from the sidelines. They think no one notices. *But Hope and I notice...* Every single time they are in a room together, you could cut the sexual tension with a damn knife.

"Oh, Ash is bringing Ava down here after her recital. She has one last performance tonight before she's on break," Aunt Lyssa says.

Ava is a dancer; she lives and breathes everything dance. She's at the top of her game right now and is the lead in her current production. Don't ask me what this one is called. I gave up keeping track of them a long time ago. I just know I'm damn proud of her. My little cousin is a dancing star.

"Okay, I'm just going to go put my things away and freshen up." And maybe lock myself in the room for a few hours until backup (AKA Hope) arrives. I cannot be the only child around the oldies. It won't be long before they start grilling me. And right now, my life is anything but perfect and put together.

I'm still at university. I'm studying for my PhD in marine biology. I love it. Everything about the ocean and ocean life... it's my jam. That part of my little world *is* perfectly sorted. I have it all planned out: I'll graduate with a PhD, then I hope to land a career in research and environmental politics, fighting for marine animals and giving the ocean a voice.

I know... *I'm a greenie.*

I walk up the stairs and into our assigned guest room, then throw my bag on the bottom bunk bed. Not much has changed since we were little girls. The paint is still the same shade of light pink. The queen-sized white bunks are set to the left, with a matching white double along the opposing wall. The room is huge. It has a large walk-in closet, which still houses some of our Christmas princess party dresses Aunt Ella refuses to throw out. There's an adjoining en suite, with a vanity table that—to this day—all three of us girls fight over for space.

Last Christmas, Ava threw a tantrum, tossing my and Hope's makeup in the trash, just so she could make room. The girl is lucky she's family.

I open the window, letting the sea breeze drift in and billow the curtains. I love the smell of the ocean, the salt, the sand. *Everything about it.* I think I developed my fascination from Aunt Ella. She's always loved the beach.

The direct view from this window is of the house next door. Or should I say of a bedroom window next door. And right now, I'm entranced by that view. I can see straight into their bathroom; the door from the bedroom has been left open. But it's the shower I can't look away from.

Not only is it an amazingly stunning bathroom, but the man currently standing under the running water, with one hand leaning against the tiled wall and the other... stroking up and down, has what looks to be one hell of an impressive cock.

My mouth waters at the sight. What I wouldn't do to jump across the windows and join him in that shower. I watch as the water droplets fall down his tanned, sculpted body. My fingers itch to follow their path. If I imagine hard enough, I can feel the firmness of those abs beneath my touch.

My eyes travel down further and get stuck watching his hand pump. His speed increases. I imagine that it's my hand wrapped around him, stroking him into a blissful mess. He turns his body slightly, his cock aimed in my direction. I look up to his face, and his eyes meet mine.

He smirks as he continues to pump himself harder. *Faster.* I don't know what's wrong with me. I can't for the life of me bring myself to look away. I'm so fucking turned on right now. Maybe I need to jump in the shower and relieve myself too. I watch as he comes; his mouth parts open slightly. I wish I could hear his voice, preferably screaming my name, as he comes undone.

He continues to stand there, washing himself off under the spray of the water and staring straight back at me. *Oh my God, do I have no shame? What the hell is wrong with me?* I just watched a complete stranger masturbate in the shower. And I'm still watching that stranger as he rubs bodywash all over himself without breaking eye contact.

His cock is still hard. I tilt my head, considering just how useful that could be to me. Biting my lip, I imagine him coming, then being ready to go again. It's not easy to find a man with that kind of stamina.

My eyes widen as I hear footsteps traveling up the stairs. I smile at him before quickly shutting the curtains and turning around, right as Hope breezes into the room and places her bag on the top bunk.

She glares at me. "What's wrong with you? Why do you look like you just got caught with your hand in the cookie jar?"

"Shut the door, Hope," I instruct her. I can't possibly keep this to myself. I've never *not* been able to share everything with her.

She narrows her eyes and swiftly closes the door. "Okay, spill. What'd you do? And how pissed off are Mum and Dad going to be?" she asks.

"Nothing—well, it wasn't my fault. I mean, who doesn't close their bathroom door? And he just had it out there, for the world to see. So, I mean, really, it's his fault, right? Oh God, Hope, I'm a bloody Peeping Tom. What if he calls the cops and tells them there's a crazy redhead next door?" I ramble on as I slump down on the bed.

"Well, they'd turn up and find not one, but three crazy redheads: you, me, and Mum. But let's backtrack. What the bloody hell are you talking about?"

"The guy from next door. No, not guy, the freaking god carved from granite stone. He was in the shower—you know, alone and... enjoying himself. I could see right into the bathroom. I watched, Hope. The whole thing. I couldn't look away. Even when he stared directly at me and finished. Like, I mean, he looked right at me, Hope. He didn't look away. I just stood there and kept watching. What kind of sick person am I?"

"I'm assuming that's a rhetorical question and not a real one," she replies as she goes to the window and pulls back the curtain.

"What the hell are you doing? Shut the curtain!" I hiss at her.

"If you can look, then so can I. Don't worry, there's no one even there. Maybe this god was just a figment of your imagination."

The thought of her staring at him like that makes me irrationally jealous. I don't want her to lust after him like I am. It's stupid. I don't even know the guy. And now, I'm going to have to spend this whole week locked up in the house, so I don't risk running into him outside on the beach. What a wasted trip this is going to be...

I get up and peek out the window. She's right. He's not there. I'm both relieved that she's not perving on him, and disappointed that I can't see him again.

2

Alex

I can't look away. The moment I saw her watching me, my cock instantly went ten times harder than it already was. The sun shone over her red hair like a fucking halo, before falling down across her pale porcelain skin. *Where the fuck did she come from?* She's fucking perfect.

And right now, my cock agrees with me. I'm struggling to contain myself as I stand here, locked in her gaze, pumping myself up and down. I come, imagining her on her knees in front of me. The vision of those luscious lips she's currently biting on wrapped around my cock.

The fact that she hasn't looked away, even after she was caught, tells me she likes what she sees just as much as I do. I give her the smirk that usually has girls weeping for me. But she's not like other girls; something deep inside me is telling me this one is different. My instincts are screaming one word: MINE. *That girl in the window is mine.* If I could reach through the glass and grab her—fucking chain her to my bed—I would.

But that house belongs to the McKinleys. I can't just storm through the door and claim what's mine. I have to be strategic about this. But one way or another, that girl is going to be mine.

We stare at each other like a game of chicken, neither one of us wanting to look away first. As I wash myself down, my cock hardens again. It's her... I've never had an issue with stamina, but this soon after coming is unusual. *Even for me.* Fuck, what do I have to do to get her in this shower with me?

Her eyes widen. She turns, looking over her shoulder before glancing back at me and smiling. Then the curtains close and she's gone. Just like that... Gone. I need to get inside that house. I need to see her again. I *will* see her again. And it will be up close next time. But like everything else in my life, I need to be strategic about claiming that girl. Fuck, I don't even know her fucking name. All I know is she's somehow connected to the McKinley family.

I throw on a pair of board shorts and head downstairs. This is more casual than I'm used to dressing, but we're at the beach, and I'm determined to give my niece a normal beachy Christmas.

"Uncle Alex, can we go build sandcastles now? Can we, can we, can we?" Tessie jumps up and down with excitement.

"Sure, we can, *bella*. Just as soon as you go get a shirt and cover up. You don't want to get burned."

"But these are my new bathers. I want to wear them. And *you* don't have a shirt on!" Tessie stands there and folds her arms over her chest.

"Well, I'm a boy. I don't need to wear a shirt. You, *little girl*, are a girl and *you* need to wear clothes," I try to explain. Even as I say it, I know it's the old school way of thinking. Usually I wouldn't give a fuck what any girl wears, unless that girl is my sister or my niece. Then I very much care.

"That's stupid. Boys are stupid. I'm not wearing a

shirt; you can't make me." Tessie is as stubborn as a fucking mule—a trait she shares with her mother.

"No, I can't make you. But I can negotiate with you. How about you put a shirt on, then we'll go outside and build the biggest and best sandcastle this town has ever seen. And when we get back inside, we'll have the biggest bowl of ice cream your stomach can handle."

"I'll be right back." She goes running up the stairs. I knew she wouldn't be able to turn down ice cream.

"Why is Tessie running up the stairs like she's being chased by the devil himself?" Mia asks as she comes out of the kitchen.

"I promised her ice cream if she went and put a shirt on." I smile, proud of my ability to negotiate with a five-year-old.

"You can't tell her she needs to cover up, Alex. She's going to develop body shame or some other body image issues. She needs to know she's beautiful and can wear whatever the hell she wants."

"She knows she's beautiful, Mia—*that's the problem.* If she weren't so beautiful, I wouldn't have to worry about the future of mankind. But, no, she had to take after you," I grumble.

"There are so many things wrong with that sentence. But I'm taking it as a compliment. So, thank you. Are you heading out to the beach with her?"

"Yeah, I proposed we build the biggest sand castle this town has ever seen."

"Great, I'm going to finish up, then I'll meet you out there."

"I'm ready. I'm ready." Tessie comes bounding down the stairs in a big fluffy princess dress. *Not exactly beach attire.*

"Ah, are you sure that's what you want to wear? You're going to get sand all over it," I ask her, confused by her choice of outfits.

"Well, I can take it off and wear my new bathers." She shrugs her shoulders at me with her hands on her hips, silently saying, "Checkmate." How the hell this level of manipulation is coming from a five-year-old, I don't know. She's too fucking smart.

"Nope, you look absolutely beautiful, *bella*. It's like I have a date with a real-life Disney princess." I offer my hand, waiting for her to take hold of it. *Counter check, little girl.*

"Last one there's a rotten egg." Tessie runs through the sliding glass door and straight out to the beach. I'm right behind her. Although, of course, she's still going to win. *How can I not let her?*

"I win! I win!" she screams as I pick her up and spin her around. Putting her down, I hold her hand as we walk along the beach collecting shells. Apparently, you need shells for decorating a sandcastle.

"What about this one?" I ask, leaning down and picking up a black shell.

"Mmm, it's okay. Maybe it could be a door handle." Tessie adds it to the bucket she's carrying.

"All right, I think we have enough shells. Let's head back and build this castle of yours."

I stand in the middle of the property line, between our residence and the McKinleys'. I can't seem to stop my eyes from straying to their porch. There're a bunch of people coming and going from inside the house. Some of them, I recognise... like Bray Williamson. The guy's a legend in the underground fight circuit.

The one person I want to get a glimpse of never comes out though. *Did I imagine her? Was she just a very realistic fantasy?* I fucking hope not. I'm so fixated on waiting for her to show I don't notice when Mia comes up behind me, slapping me over the head and shocking me out of my stupor. I immediately pivot on my heel. Anyone else... and I would have them in a choke hold right now.

"You're lucky I love you," I grunt at her.

"Why are you staring at the neighbours? What are you up to, Alex?" she asks.

"Nothing. I'm just taking in my surroundings. In

case you didn't notice, we're on a beach—*without weapons*. We're literally sitting ducks right now, Mia."

She looks around. "I can count ten of your men, without even straining too hard. They think they're blending in. But that one over there." She points to the silhouette closest to the water. "He's been waxing that surfboard for two hours."

"Well, maybe it needs a lot of wax," I retort. She's right though. They're meant to be blending in better. I'm going to have to have words with them.

"It's starting to get dark; we should head inside and get stuck into that ice cream, Tessie."

"Yes!" She squeals as she stands, before jumping up and down on the castle we just spent the last hour making.

"Why'd you destroy it?" I ask.

"It's the fun part." She laughs.

I notice Leo nod his head at me as he approaches us. "Mia, take Tessie in and get her that bowl of ice cream I promised her, please."

"Come on, *bella*. Let's go eat our feelings," Mia says.

"Mummy, you can't eat feelings," the little girl counters as they walk away.

I wait until they're out of earshot before I speak. "What's up?" I ask Leo.

"The shipment from Bali has gone missing," he says.

"What do you mean *missing*? How the fuck does a shipping container just go missing?" I growl. I'd love to fucking yell and scream right now, but I'm on a goddamn public beach.

"There's no trace of it. The escorts are unreachable —we haven't been able to make contact with a single one."

"Find it, and find *them*. I want their fucking heads. Whoever thought they could steal from me... I want their fucking heads on a spike. That's a 1.5 million dollar shipment, Leo. Fucking find it." I storm off inside the house.

"I'm working on it!" he shouts after me.

He doesn't follow though. He's been with me long enough to know when to keep his distance. And right now, everyone in the fucking vicinity needs to keep their fucking distance.

I've been sitting here in the dark for hours, just hoping to get another glimpse of her through the window. I'm fuming about my missing shipment. I've reached out to every port authority I have on the books, and no one can tell me where the fuck my container is.

I bring my glass to my lips and sip at the whiskey—my old mate, Jack Daniels, usually helps with anything. But right now, he's not doing *jack* shit.

I continue to watch the window like a fucking stalker. And similar to how I had been watching the front porch, I've seen plenty of people come and go from that bedroom. I even saw one who looked just like her, and for a minute, I thought she was *her*. But she wasn't *her*. I didn't feel that connection I felt earlier when I looked at my mystery woman—her smile wasn't as bright.

Tomorrow is going to be a better day. Tomorrow, I'm going to figure out how to get inside that house and find my girl. I'm just about to give up and turn in for the night when she appears in the window. She's looking into the darkness of my room.

She seems a little lost, as if she is unsure why she's even standing there. I flick on the table lamp next to me, illuminating myself. I want her to see me. Her mouth opens, and I can almost hear her gasp as she stares back at me.

Leaning forward, I rest my arms on my knees as I take in her beauty. I could sit here all night and stare at her. She's a fucking siren, a beacon calling out to my soul.

She smiles shyly as she pulls the curtains closed on me again, blocking my view for the second time today. At least now I know she's fucking real, and I was not imagining that shit.

3

Lily

I tossed and turned all night. I feel slightly hung over this morning, and I didn't even drink last night. Every time I closed my eyes, I kept seeing him. *The Adonis from the window.* The image of him pleasuring himself played on repeat, like a broken track. Then there was that intense stare he gave me...

The last thing I expected when I looked out into the darkness was to see him sitting in a chair staring straight back at me. His room was dark. Then, out of nowhere, a light turned on, showing him sitting there in a pair of black briefs with a whisky glass in one hand. It's almost like he was waiting for me to make an appearance. But that's a ridiculous notion. Men like that do not wait around for girls like me.

When he leaned forward, resting his elbows on his knees, I felt that stare pierce straight through to my soul. Like something physically clicked inside me. A magnet trying to pull me closer to him. I wish I could meet him somewhere my family wasn't. Don't get me wrong... I love my family, but there is no way I'm bringing any guy I'm interested in around them.

I think I'll wait until I have a ring on my finger before I do that. At least then, he's somewhat locked in, and my dad and uncles can't kill him. That's my theory anyway. Maybe Hope or Ava can bring a boy home first. Get the shock of us girls being grown-ass women out of the way before it's my turn.

I didn't date much in high school. I was focused on my studies, to make sure I got into the course I wanted at university. But once I left high school, turned eighteen, and started going out... well, let's just say that interest in guys evolved hard and fast. I've been on more first dates than I can remember. I've had a whole of two serious boyfriends, each lasting only a couple of months.

Once they found out who my family was, they ran scared. Not literally, but the relationships always went downhill shortly after discovering that little tidbit of information. And that's before they even heard about the extended side...

I'll never understand what they saw. Deep down, we're a normal family. Sure, my parents are successful, but they've both worked their asses off to earn what they have.

Throwing the blankets off, I decide to make a start for the day. I can already hear the commotion downstairs. I bang on the bathroom door and yell out, "Ava, how long are you going to be? I need to pee."

"Beauty is time, Lily. Not all of us are blessed like you and Hope. Some of us have to work to look good," she yells back.

Like hell she has to work. That girl is a walking bloody Barbie. She has the tanned Williamson skin, and the blonde hair and blue eyes of Aunt Lyssa. Pair that with her little dancer's body and you have a fucking real-life doll.

I head into the hall to use the main bathroom. I'm not waiting for the hours it's going to take Ava to finish in there. As I'm exiting the bathroom, my dad's stepping out of the bedroom he and my mum are staying in.

"Sweetheart, what's wrong? Are you sick?" he asks, kissing my forehead.

"No, just tired," I grumble, leaning into his embrace.

"Let's go find some coffee, preferably before your

mother attempts to make it again, like she did last Christmas."

"Argh, don't even. I can still taste the horror. I don't understand it. How is she even related to Gran? I really wish she had inherited some cooking skills," I say, remembering my Gran's baked goods.

"You and me both, Lil. Damn, that woman can bake."

"Mmm, maybe I'll bake something to take to her and Pops tomorrow," I think out loud.

"I'm sure she'd love that," my dad replies.

Walking into the kitchen, I note that Uncle Zac is at the coffee machine. "Uncle Zac, can you make me an almond cap? Please," I ask in the sweetest voice I can muster as I sit at the counter.

"Sure can, Lily Pilly. Right after I make Aunt Lyssa's coffee."

I don't recall a morning where I've slept at my aunt and uncle's, and he hasn't made Aunt Lyssa's coffee. It's cute how much he cares for her. All the men in my family really have set the bar so high I'm not sure I'll ever find a man who can measure up to their level. The respect they each have for my aunts, and the way my dad loves my mum and isn't afraid to show it, no matter who's around... it's the stuff fairy tales are made of. As much as I complain about it grossing me out, I secretly pray I will find a man who loves me like that.

The image of the man from the window pops in my head again.

"Here you go," Uncle Zac says, placing a steamy mug of coffee in front of me. I look up into the scrutinising gazes of both my dad and my uncle.

"Oh, fuck... Bray, for the love of God, tell me you've still got that left hook of yours," Uncle Zac grunts.

"You still prepared to get your hands dirty?" my dad counters.

"Fuck yes, I am. Think Josh will let us feed the pigs?" Uncle Zac says.

I'm confused as hell. "What the hell are you two going on about? Is it that time already? The dementia kicking in? Should I go get Aunt Lyssa?"

My dad props himself against the counter, his elbows wide and his face eye-level with mine. "Who is he? What's his name, Lily?"

"Who?" I ask, still having no idea what they're going on about.

"Don't play dumb, Lil. You're way too smart for it. Who's the guy who put that look on your face just now?"

"I have no idea what you are talking about." *Deny, deny, deny.* I repeat the mantra in my head. No matter how hard he tries, my dad can't actually see into my thoughts.

"I know that look, Lily. It's the look your mother gets when she thinks about your dad, the same look your Aunt Ella gets whenever Uncle Dean walks into a room. I *know* that look."

"Call Dean and Josh. We're going to need an inter-rogation room," my dad announces.

"No, you're not. There's no guy—*sorry*. My life is boring." I get up to walk away. Remembering my coffee mug, I turn back and pick it up. "And if there were, there is no way in hell I'd tell either of you about him."

"You know I'll find out anyway," Uncle Zac says.

I ignore him and head out to the back deck. Finding a comfy deck chair, I settle in and sip my coffee while watching the waves roll in and out. They're both wrong. I can't have that look over a guy I don't even know. I don't even have a name for him.

Not five minutes later, my dad comes out and sits on the chair next to me.

"Lily, you know you can talk to me about anything, right? I know I may come across as overbearing... *at times*."

I laugh into my mug. At times? *Yeah, right.*

"Okay, most times. But that's only because you're my little girl. You will always be my little girl. No matter how old you get."

"Thanks, Dad."

"If there is a guy you're interested in, you should bring him around. I'll be on my best behaviour. I'll rein in your uncles. But, if he does something I don't like, doesn't treat you right, all bets are off."

"There is no guy, Dad. Well, there might be. I don't know yet. How did you know that Mum was the one for you? When did you know?"

"I knew from the moment I saw her... It's corny as fuck. But when I looked at her, I just knew there would never be anyone else but her. Did I ever tell you about the time your mum tried to dodge me by switching clothes with Aunt Holly?"

I shake my head no. My mum is one half a twin too. My Aunt Holly is living in New York with her hunky Italian husband. They have four sons: Theo, Matteo, Romeo and Luca. My Aunt Holly's husband is—well, we don't say it out loud—but he's a Don, the head of a mafia family. My cousins are all following in their father's footsteps and entering the family business.

"They both came out the lift. Your mum tried to walk straight past me, dressed as Aunt Holly. I took her in my arms and kissed the hell out of her. She couldn't resist my charm, of course."

"Of course, who could?" I retort with an eye roll.

"Anyway, your mum realised she was meant to be Holly, and got mad. Started yelling at me. But you see, *I knew*. From the moment they stepped out of the lift, I knew. When I look at your mum, I still get butterflies. When I look at Aunt Holly, that never happens. Even though they look exactly the same."

"Okay, so I just need to find a guy, put myself and Hope in a room together, and see if he can tell which one I am?"

"Not exactly that method, Lil. You need to find someone who will physically ache without you. Someone who will move heaven and earth for you. I want you to find a love that gives you butterflies, still, twenty years later."

"What if that never happens for me, Dad?"

"It will happen. In the meantime, don't ever settle for anything less."

My dad's arm flies up, catching a ball that was heading straight for my face. "Nice reflexes." I laugh.

"Like a cat. Looks like your old man's still got it."

"Shit... Ah, hi. Sorry, my niece, Tessie..." The guy—no, the god from the window—points over his shoulder at a little girl in a princess dress. "She got a little carried away. Didn't know she had that kind of an arm on her. Ah, I'm Alex." He holds out a hand to my dad, but his gaze doesn't leave mine.

"Bray." My dad shakes his hand. I can see the pressure he's enacting. Alex looks at my dad but doesn't back down. I elbow Dad in the ribs, probably harder than I needed to. He glances at me and laughs. Breaking the handshake, he says, "This is Lily. My daughter." With an emphasis on the word *daughter*. Can the world please swallow me whole now?

I look up towards the sky, waiting for the apocalypse. Please, just let this be the end, so I don't have to face the embarrassment of this situation.

4

Alex

*L*ily, her name is Lily. Fitting, because her beauty is as sweet and innocent as a lily flower. Following her line of sight, I look up. *What the hell is she looking for?* There's nothing to see but blue skies.

"Are you looking for something in particular?" I ask, smiling at her.

"Just waiting for the apocalypse." She shrugs as she stands. Bray laughs beside her.

"Uncle Alex, did you get my ball?" Tessie comes up, hugging my leg. For a little girl with so much confidence, she's shy around new people. More reason to homeschool her, I think.

"I sure did. Here you go, *bella*." I hand her the pink beach ball.

Tessie stares at Lily. "Are you a real-life princess?" she asks her. *Told you...* She's fucking beautiful, even my five-year-old niece thinks so.

"Um, no, I'm not. But if you were to ask my dad or my uncles, they'd probably say otherwise." Lily bends over to Tessie's level, giving me a view straight down her fucking tank top. It takes everything in me not to stare at her breasts. But getting a hard-on, in front of her dad, the first time I meet him is not how our story is going to start.

"I'm Lily. It's nice to meet you. Are *you* a real-life princess?" Lily whispers.

"Well, my Uncle Alex says I'm his princess. But I don't have a daddy so I'm not sure," Tessie says so matter-of-factly.

"You know what? I'm one hundred percent certain your Uncle Alex is right. Because you sure do look like a real-life princess to me," Lily answers her perfectly, not mentioning the "I don't have a daddy" part of Tessie's speech.

"I'm Tessie. And I think you look like a princess too.

Doesn't she look beautiful, like a princess, Uncle Alex?" Tessie tugs on my hand to get my attention.

"She sure does, *bella*."

Lily straightens, a red hue rising up over her cheeks. "Ah, thanks?" she questions.

Bray raises his eyebrows at Lily before turning to me. "Alex, we're having a pre-Christmas Eve barbecue tonight. The entire family will be here. Why don't you guys come and join us?" he asks me, but we're both looking at Lily's wide-eyed reaction.

"Sure, we'd love to, wouldn't we, Tessie?"

"Will there be ice cream?" Tessie asks.

"I'm sure we can dig some up. What's your favourite flavour?" Bray responds.

"Chocolate. And vanilla—oh! And strawberry," Tessie rattles off. Before she can add more requests, I interrupt.

"She likes them all," I tell him.

"That's because they're all great." Bray winks at Tessie, causing her to laugh.

"Coming! Be there in a sec," Lily yells towards the house. I look to the door, but there's no one to be seen. "Sorry, nice to meet you, Tessie. I gotta go inside—my mum's calling me." She tries to walk around me, but I purposefully step in front of her, so she has to look up.

"It was nice to meet you too, Lily." I smile, before stepping out of her way and watching her run off.

Bray stands there, staring at me, with his arms folded over his chest. I can see my men spread out on the beach, watching and waiting to intervene. Closing my left hand as discreetly as I can, I hold out one finger. It's a sign for them to stand down. Bray doesn't miss the action. He quirks his eyebrow at me. I can tell he wants to say something, but he's holding back because of Tessie's presence.

"*Bella*, go see if you can beat Uncle Leo in a slug race. Winner gets the biggest bowl." Without a thought, Tessie runs off, yelling out for Leo. I watch until Leo catches her. Once she's safely in his arms, I turn my attention back to Bray. I wait for him to speak. It doesn't take long.

"If you hurt her, you're going to need more than *them* to save your ass, Alessandro." I don't let my shock manifest outwardly. He knows who I am...

"Wouldn't dream of hurting her, Mr. Williamson," I answer him.

"Great. Good to see we are on the same page. I'm assuming you can handle yourself around her fucking crazy uncles. I'm looking forward to this barbecue even more now."

I'm confused as fuck. If he knows who I am, then why is he letting me around his family? It doesn't make sense. Unless he wants something from me... What that could be, I have no fucking idea. "You clearly know who I am. Why aren't you running me off your porch right now? Most fathers would have a gun to my head, warning me to stay away from their daughter. Why aren't you?"

"Would it make any difference if I did?" he asks.

"Fuck no, but you could always try." I smirk.

"I may not like it, but I know that look my daughter had when she saw you. I saw it earlier this morning too. Have you met my daughter before today?"

"Not officially. I saw her in passing yesterday." I won't go into detail on how we were *unofficially* introduced—that memory will go to the grave with me.

"Right, well, good luck... You're going to need it. Come to dinner unarmed. My wife's not fond of guns."

"As you can clearly see, I don't walk around armed everywhere I go, sir. But yes. I'll be sure to leave the goons at home." He nods his head as he walks inside.

Fuck, what the fuck kind of mind-fuckery was that? I'm not sure if he just challenged me, or gave me his fucking blessing to chase after his daughter.

I head back down to the beach. Tonight is going to be interesting. *That's for sure.*

"Boss, I've found the missing container—it's been emptied. Apart from the two bodies left rotting inside it, that is," Leo says, entering my study.

Fuck. I throw my glass across the room. "How the fuck did this happen? I want names, Leo. I want their fucking families' names. Their friends' names."

"We're tracking CCTV footage of the docks now. The container came in on a ship owned by the Houghten Group. I'm tracking the company to see who the fuck runs it. The paperwork is leading me down a rabbit hole. It's operated under a shell corporation. But I'll find the trail; there's always a trail."

"Good, keep following it." I look at my watch. It's almost six. We didn't agree on specifics, but it's universally known that 6 p.m. is the time to turn up. Also, I'm fucking anxious as hell to see her again. "Mia, Tessie, and I will be going next door for dinner," I say out loud.

"Wait, back the fuck up. I thought you just said you were going to the McKinleys' for dinner."

"That's exactly what I just said."

"Why? You can't go in there and piss that family off. There's a lot riding on this merger, and last I checked, Joshua McKinley doesn't exactly like you very much already. What makes you think eating dinner with his family is going to get you in his good graces."

"Because I'm charming as hell?" I suggest.

"No, you're not. I really hope you know what you're doing."

"I don't, but when have I ever led us astray, Leo?"

"Never. Which is why I never question your

instincts. But just… be careful. I've heard disturbing shit about Joshua McKinley."

"More disturbing than the shit you've seen me actually do?" I question.

"No, you're right. I don't know what the hell I'm worried about. Two psychos in one room, what could possibly go wrong?"

"Nothing's going to go wrong. Besides, Tessie will be there. That child can win the heart of the coldest of men."

I walk out and knock on Mia's door before opening it. She's bending down, tying Tessie's shoe. "Are my two favourite girls ready?" I ask. As I say the words, I realise I have another favourite girl to add to the list.

I make a mental note to get Leo to add a security detail to Lily. As soon as word is out that I'm interested in her, she will become a target. The thought of something happening to her sends me cold. I won't let anyone touch her. They will have to get through me first.

"I'm ready. Let's go. Do you think Lily will like my princess dress?" Tessie asks.

"Do you like your princess dress, *bella*?" I counter.

"It's my favourite." She beams.

"Then, that's all that matters. You don't dress to impress other people, Tessie. You dress for you and only you," I tell her.

"Well, I also like my new bathers, so I'm wearing them tomorrow to the beach."

I go to backtrack, but Mia shuts me up. "Baby girl, you can wear anything you want to the beach. I'll go in the water with you tomorrow. I have a new bikini I want to wear too."

"Why couldn't you have been a brother?" I ask, only getting a laugh in response.

"Let's go! I want to see Lily!" Tessie runs down the stairs as fast as she can in the big dress.

"Who's this Lily I haven't stopped hearing about?" Mia prompts.

"The lady from next door," I answer. I'm not ready to divulge my plans of Lily becoming *my* Lily. There's always that niggling thought in the back of my mind, that I should keep my distance from her, protect her from my world. I'm currently at the top of the Sydney underworld. I have multiple enemies—families fighting for power, fighting to take what's mine. But as much as I should stay away from the girl next door, I can't seem to keep my distance.

"Tessie, wait up. Don't open the door by yourself," I yell out, racing down the steps to stop my overly excited niece from running outside alone. I know she wouldn't really be alone. There're men stationed all around this house, hidden in the darkness of the shadows.

"Well, hurry, Uncle Alex." I get to the door and pick her up.

"How about I carry you, so your princess shoes don't get sand in them."

"Good idea," she agrees.

"Alex, why *exactly* are we making friends with the neighbours?" Mia asks.

"Why not?"

"We never have before."

"Well, times are changing, sis. Just go with the flow. No family business talk. You know the drill." I don't need to remind her. Mia and I have looked after each other our whole lives. There's only a fourteen-month age difference between us. Let's just say our parents should never have been parents. It's always been Mia and me, against the world. Then Leo came into the fold when I was thirteen.

"Sure. Don't worry, with the number of hot male specimens I've seen coming and going from that house the past two days, I'll be too busy trying not to physically drool."

"Gross." I shiver at the thought of my sister lusting after anyone. I know she clearly does; we wouldn't have Tessie otherwise. But that doesn't mean I have to like the idea.

There's a heap of people sitting on the deck, and some out on the beach around a little bonfire.

"Hi, I'm Alex. This is my sister, Mia. And my niece, Tessie. Bray invited us." I introduce myself to whom I know from my research is Ella McKinley.

"Hi, welcome. Please come in. I'm Ella. Hold on a sec." She sticks her head through the door and yells out, "Bray, get your ass outside. Your guests are here."

Tessie wiggles in my arms. "Let me down, Uncle Alex. Let me down." I put her on her feet and watch as she takes off across the deck.

"Lily, Lily, do you like my princess dress?" she squeals excitedly. I follow her.

"I'm sorry," I say to the confused girl sitting in the deck chair. "Tessie, that's not Lily."

Tessie looks from me to the Lily lookalike, and back again. Her eyes narrow. The whole deck has gone quiet.

Shit, did I say something wrong already?

5

Oh my God, I heard Tessie calling out my name so I stepped outside just as Alex tells her that Hope is not me. How the hell did he know that from just looking at her? She didn't even talk. She's just sitting there, as stunned as I am.

That never happens. Strangers don't know the difference. God, half the time, Ash can't even tell us apart, and he's been around us our whole lives.

"Yes, it is. We met her this morning, Uncle Alex. Don't you remember?" Tessie whispers.

"I remember, *bella*, but this isn't Lily. Trust me. This is…?" Alex looks to my twin for the answer.

"Ah, Hope. I'm Hope. I'm Lily's sister, twin sister. It's nice to meet you, Tessie," she says.

"Hope? Twin? What's a twin, Uncle Alex?" Tessie asks.

"It's when a mummy has two babies at the same time."

"Two. There are two real-life princesses here?" Tessie continues.

"I guess so," Alex says as his eyes land on mine, sending me that panty-melting smile of his. Everyone is staring, watching.

Except my dad, who loudly declares, "Told you so." And everyone laughs.

"Alex, this is my wife—Reilly." My dad introduces mum. What kind of alternate universe did I wake up in this morning?

"Hello, ma'am."

"It's Reilly, not ma'am. I'm not that old. Do I look that old?" Mum asks him.

"No, Reilly. Not at all. Ah, this is my sister—Mia." I watch as he pulls Mia over to him, like he's her shield.

"Hi, thanks for having us over. Tessie has been so excited all afternoon," Mia says.

"Oh, it's our pleasure."

"Grab a seat. Make yourself comfortable. What would you like to drink?" My mum asks.

"Water's fine. Thank you," Alex answers as he continues to stare at me. I can't handle it. I don't know what voodoo he has on me. I don't understand why he's not running for the hills yet, or why my dad hasn't chased him off.

Alex makes no attempt to hide the fact that he's looking at me. He did it this morning too. I just want the world to swallow me up.

"Lily!" Tessie spots me. She stops in front of me. "You are Lily, right?" she asks, and everyone laughs again.

"Yes, sweetie, I am. You are Tessie, right? I almost thought you were Cinderella. I was waiting for Prince Charming to turn up with your glass slipper." I bend down to speak to her.

"No, silly, I'm Tessie. Look, I still have both shoes." She pulls up the bottom of her huge princess dress to show me two very sparkly shoes.

"Well, Tessie, I'm about to go and sit by the fire. Would you like to join me?" I ask her.

"Oh, sorry. She's a bad asthmatic. She can't get too close to the smoke. Hi, I'm Mia." Alex's sister holds her hand out to me. This girl is beautiful beyond words. Dark, tanned skin. Dark hair. Flawless features. And her cheekbones... what I wouldn't pay to have those cheekbones.

"Hi, sorry. I didn't know." I shake her outstretched

48

hand.

"No worries. Tessie, come and sit with me for a bit, baby." Mia leads her over to a deck chair by Hope, and they both sit down. Everyone else has gone back to chattering amongst themselves. Alex is still talking to my parents about God knows what. His eyes travel between them and me, almost like he's pleading for me to come and save him. I smile back at him.

Nope, I'm out of here. Ash, Bree, and Axel are all sitting around the fire. That's where I'm heading, to the safety of my cousins. They can keep me busy, so I don't make more of a fool of myself.

I take off my coverall and place it on the sand before I sit down. There's nothing worse than sitting on the beach and ending up with sand everywhere. I'm wearing a black string bikini underneath, and I'm on the beach, so I figure when in Rome... The sun is just setting. It's still daylight, but it's dimming.

The air is cooling down after a scorching day. I try to stay out of the sun as much as possible, preferring to come out to the beach in the early hours of the morning or in the evening, when I'm not going to end up looking like a damn lobster.

"Really, Lily? You couldn't find any clothes to put on?" Ash strips his shirt off, throwing it over the top of the little bonfire and onto me. "Put that on," he grunts.

"You sound like Uncle Zac." I toss the shirt back. I'm not putting that on. I look to Bree, who is also wearing a coverall. I know she'll be sporting a hot-ass bikini underneath it. I silently plead with her to join me. Girl power and all. It doesn't take long before she winks in my direction.

"You know what? I think Lily is onto something, sitting on the sand instead of these beach chairs." She stands and moves her fold-out chair behind her. She then makes a show of wiggling out of her coverall, unveiling a gorgeous, royal-blue, two-piece bikini.

"What the fuck, Bree? No!" Ash growls.

"Yes!" she says back as she sits down.

"Axe, help me out here, would you?" Ash complains to his brother.

"Sorry, mate, you're on your own. I'm all about empowering women. They can wear what they like. It's not like anyone's actually going to hit on them here." Axe waves his arms around.

I feel *him* before I see him. He drops down next to me, almost on top of me. Without saying a word, he pulls his shirt over the back of his head. Handing it to me, he says, "You look cold. Put it on."

Ah, excuse me? What in the hell? Who does he think he is? I'm at a loss for words over his boldness. He may be hot as fuck, and those abs... They might be carved from stone and have me sitting on my hands to prevent myself from reaching out. But he does not get to tell me what to do.

I tilt my head and glare at him. He doesn't budge and instead continues to hold the shirt out to me, like it's a sure thing I'm going to take it.

"Oh, man. This is going to be good. Give him hell, Lil!" Axe hoots.

"Lily, want me to call the cleaners? You know, just to be prepared by the time you're done ripping his balls off. I can have them here and ready in about twenty minutes," Breanna jokes. At least, I think she's joking... She says shit like this all the time, so I honestly don't know.

Alex glances over to her. "There won't be a need for cleaners." He looks back to me. "Lily, sweetheart, it's getting chilly. I'd very much hate for you to catch a cold on Christmas. What kind of neighbour would I be if I didn't do something to prevent that from happening?"

"Oh, shit, Lily, don't cave. Stand strong, girl," Axe says, resulting in Alex sending him a death glare.

"Is he someone important to you, Lily?" Alex asks me while staring at Axe.

"My cousin, so I should probably say yes." I laugh.

"Right, unfortunate..." he mumbles, returning his expectant eyes to me.

"Lily, you should take the shirt. Remember last Christmas, when you and Hope spent most of the night outside and you both ended up sick all Christmas day. The whole family caught your cold," Ash, not so helpfully, adds in his two cents.

"Ash, shut up." I point over to him. "Also a cousin, but suddenly way less important."

Alex smirks at me. "That one, I think I like." He

reaches a hand over to Ash. "I'm Alex. The new neighbour."

"Ash—the cousin she loves the most." Ash laughs.

"Well, it's great you two can be friends and chat. Lord knows Ash could use some friends. He works far too much. I'm going for a swim. Want to come, Bree?" I ask.

She shakes her head. Bree's never been a fan of the ocean. "I'd rather have my toenails ripped off one by one with a pair of rusty tweezers," she responds.

"There is something seriously wrong with you," I tell her, rising to my feet.

"Wait, you're not seriously going out there, now, are you?" Alex asks me.

"Yes, why not?"

"Because it's getting dark. How are you going to see a shark coming, or a jellyfish? Do you know how many things can kill you in that water?"

"Actually, *I do.* But don't worry, the box jellyfish is the worst, and they reside up the north end of Australia."

"Fine, if you're determined to put yourself in unnecessary danger, I'll go with you." He gets up and nods his head, and out of nowhere, a man appears. Alex passes him his phone, takes his wallet out of his pocket, and removes his watch, handing them all to this guy, who then slinks back to wherever it was he was hiding.

"Friend of yours?" I ask Alex. I look around at my

cousins. Surely, I'm not alone in thinking that exchange was odd; however, Axe is the only one who seems the least bit confused. I've also been around my Aunty Holly enough to know a 'family friend' when I see one.

"Something like that. Let's go." Alex takes hold of my hand, like it's the most natural thing in the world to do. The spark that runs up my arm at the contact makes me pull back. But Alex just holds on tighter, leading me down into the ocean. As soon as the cool water hits our feet, he stops. "Are you sure you have to do this now? We can come back out here tomorrow. You know, when it's daylight." He really doesn't want to go in.

I smile at him. "You don't have to follow me to my death, Alex. I'm more than capable of swimming out here by myself."

"Your death is not something to joke about, Lily." His jaw clenches as he gets out the words.

"You don't even know me. Why would you care?"

"I don't know why, but I do. So, if you're going in, then I'm coming."

I drop his hand and start running into the waves. "It's your choice, Alex," I call out. As soon as I get into the waist-deep water, I dive in. Coming back up, I open my eyes to a very pissed off looking Alex. "What's wrong? Did you get stung? Bitten?" I ask him. Shit, now that he's in here, what if he does get stung or something and it's my fault.

"No, but I did almost die from a fucking heart attack when it took you so long to come back up."

I laugh. "*This*, being in the ocean, is like a second home to me."

"Why?" He screws his face up.

"I've always loved it." I duck under the water again. His hands dive in and are on me quicker than I can swim away.

He tugs me to the surface, pulling my body tightly against his. My hands lean on his chest. As I blink my eyes open, I'm met with his dark brown ones. He's even more beautiful up close. He reaches a hand forward and brushes the wet hair from my face.

6

Alex

"I thought I must have imagined you. That I created the ultimate fantasy in my head, and you weren't real," I whisper, not intending for her to hear my thoughts.

Her smile, shy, small, yet still visible makes my stomach turn with a million butterflies. "How fast can you run?" she asks.

"Pretty fast if I had to. Why?"

"Because of what I'm about to do, right here." She looks back to the house where her family is spread out on the deck and along the beach. "You might just have to run for your life."

I don't get the chance to ask her what she's talking about before her lips crash into mine. The instant our mouths fuse together, everything else is gone. The people, the thoughts of tiny critters eating me alive in the ocean… it all goes.

The only thing I can focus on is *more*. I want more. I pull her tighter against me, and her legs swing around and encircle my waist. "Argh," I groan into her mouth as I take ownership of this kiss. She may have been the one to initiate it, but I'll be the one to possess it. And her.

My hands squeeze the flesh of her ass, pushing her core right up against my hard cock. The little sighs and moans she makes into my mouth egg me on to explore further. We're waist-deep in water. Nobody can see what's happening beneath the surface. I also haven't been shot in the back yet, so I'm assuming either her family isn't watching, or they aren't going to fight me on this.

My fingers push aside the fabric covering her pussy; they are twitching at the thought of entering her, of bringing her to ecstasy. The tips of my fingers lightly pad over her nub, and her whole body jolts in my arms. I smile into her mouth as our tongues continue to duel with each other. Each time my hand runs over that sensitive spot, she shivers and her legs tighten around me. I love how responsive she is. My fingers travel down before one slowly pushes into her. She goes rigid as she pulls away from my mouth. My movements halt, waiting to see what caused her to go so cold all of a sudden.

"Alex, we shouldn't. I mean, we can't do this here. My family's right there. *My dad* is right there. We can't." She shakes her head and tries to unwrap her legs from my waist. My hands move quickly to hold them in place.

"We can, and we very much should." I pull her pussy hard against my cock. She curses under her breath.

"I'm sorry. I can't." She looks back to the house. I follow her gaze; nobody is paying us any mind. They are all busy, mingling amongst each other. Scanning the beach, where I know each of my men are stationed, I see that most of them are respectfully averting their eyes. Except for one, who appears to have his phone directed our way. When I see the flash of light going off in his hands, I know for sure he's taking photos of us.

My blood boils and my jaw clenches. My hard-on is gone in an instant as I plot all the ways I'm going to torture this fucker. "You know what? You're right. We shouldn't be doing this out in public. Nobody but me should get to see you when I make you come so hard you pass out. Over and over again." I lean in and kiss her gently. I can't let myself get carried away. "Come on, let's get out of here. It's getting cold. I'd hate for you to get sick on Christmas." I walk out of the ocean with Lily in my arms. Steve, a member of my security detail, approaches with two towels.

I take one and wrap it around Lily. It kills me that I'm about to send her back up to the house alone. Fuck, that's a really fucking bad look. I was planning on dealing with the dipshit who thought he could take pictures of us in the water.

Turning back to Steve, I lean in and quietly tell him to do whatever he has to do to get that fucker tied to a chair in the basement of my house. He agrees, then hands me the second towel, along with my phone and wallet.

I dial Leo. He's about the only one I trust to get that phone and make sure those pictures never see the light of day. Taking Lily's palm, I slowly lead her back up the beach, while putting the call through to Leo with my other hand. He answers almost immediately. "You fucked up, didn't you? What's the damage?" he says.

"No, I fucking didn't, idiot. Steve's bringing someone back to the house. I need you to go through the fucker's phone. Delete any and all traces of the pictures that were taken tonight. Make sure they haven't already been sent or uploaded somewhere. I want them gone, Leo."

"Ah, sure, boss. Care to explain why you're walking up the beach, holding hands with one of the hot-ass Williamson twins?" he pries.

My hand wraps around the phone as I glance up towards my house. Sure enough, Leo is standing on the balcony. He's looking right at me. "No, I don't. And watch your fucking mouth, asshole. I will cut your goddamn tongue out if you speak about her like that again." I hang up. *Fuck.*

I look over to Lily, who is staring at me wide-eyed. Her steps halt. "Who the hell are you?" she asks.

I smile. I knew this conversation was coming, I just didn't anticipate it being this soon. Maybe I can get out of it by being vague. "I'm Alex. Remember? We met this morning?"

"Don't be coy. What is it that you do for a living, Alex?"

"Business."

"Oh yeah, what kind of business?" She pulls her hand free from mine and crosses her arms over her chest, waiting for an answer.

"I have multiple businesses; we really don't have time to discuss all of them right now. If you'd like, I can have my assistant email you a directory, containing a list of each of my companies." *I'm an asshole.* I know I sound like a pretentious dick. But I don't think she's ready to hear about the darker side of my professional dealings yet.

"That's not necessary. Why do you have so many men just following you around?"

"Security. You can never be too careful, Lily." I shrug my shoulders.

"I know you're not telling me everything. I'm not stupid, Alex. Maybe when you decide you're man enough to tell me who you actually are, we can talk again. Until then, have a great night."

She storms off towards the house. I follow her, swiping up her discarded dress and shaking the sand off along the way. I'm both in awe and fucking pissed off at her right now. I admire that she basically just told me to shove my bullshit where the sun doesn't shine. And fucking fuming because she basically just told me to shove my bullshit where the sun doesn't shine.

No one speaks to me like that—*ever.* The ones who have tried quickly regret it. But here she is, a little firecracker of perfection, and she's telling me where to go. That being said, all that comes to mind right now is that this woman has the power to fucking destroy me. And that knowledge is unsettling.

7

Lily

Oh my God, I can't believe I just let this total stranger almost finger me in the fucking ocean... in front of my family. *What was I thinking?* I wasn't. I was letting my vagina do all the thinking for me, and boy did she want to be petted by his fingers.

Damn it, that traitorous bitch still wants his fingers on her. *In her*. His mouth would work too, the way his tongue was fighting with mine. I can only imagine the kind of pleasure that tongue could bring me if it took a trip downtown.

No, I will not be imagining that. The asshole couldn't even give me an answer as to what he does for work. Business! *Pishh*, what kind of answer is that? An arrogant jerk answer is what it is.

Maybe he doesn't want to tell me because he's hiding more than just what he does for a living. Does he have a wife and kids somewhere? The more I think about it, the more questions I have.

He has men just standing around watching, like they're waiting for an attack or something. They seem to appear with just the nod of his head, ready to be at his beck and call. Well, if he thinks I'm going to be one of his little minions, he can think again.

Storming onto the deck, I find Hope sitting at the long bench table. I plop myself next to her, steal the wine glass out of her hand, and down the entire thing. Reaching over the table for the bottle, I refill the glass and sip at the cool wine.

"Ah, I wasn't drinking that anyway," Hope says to me, picking up another glass.

"Sorry, but I really freaking needed that."

I feel his presence as he sits beside me. I make it a point to not look in his direction. I can feel everyone's eyes on me, watching my every move. I don't like it.

"Okay, what'd you do?" Hope says to Alex, bending around in front of me so she can see him.

"Me? Nothing," he answers her. "Lily, you left your

dress on the beach. You should put it on." He places my discarded clothing on the table in front of me.

I look up. My dad is sitting across from me, along with Uncle Zac and Josh. My dad is smirking while rubbing his hands together. "I've got a hundred on Lil," he says.

"My money's on the new guy," Uncle Zac counters.

"Lily, sweetheart, I'll pay you one million if you let me watch as you tear his balls from his body. I'll even let you feed the pigs," Josh adds.

"What? I have no idea what any of you are talking about," I say, holding my head high before turning to Alex. "One million is a lot of money, and he's good for it. So, I'm most definitely considering this offer. Do you know how far one million dollars will go in aiding the Marine Conservation Society?"

"No, I don't, but I'm sure you do. Lily, if you want to donate a million dollars to the ocean, I'll wire the money into your account right now." He pulls his phone out and starts tapping away. He's not actually going to... Oh shit, I know it's rude, but I can't help myself. As I hear the ping go off on his phone, I snatch it out of his hand and stare at the screen.

"You didn't! Why would you do that? Are you nuts? Oh my God, wait... How did you have my bank account details?"

"I didn't. I had your phone number, which is listed publicly, by the way. Any weirdo can track you down using that."

63

"But this is a million dollars, Alex. Take it back." I return his phone.

"Lily, donate it to your charity. It seems important to you, which means it's now important to me."

"Huh, what else is important to you?" I ask him. I don't know how he does it, but when I talk to him, I get so lost in those dark eyes of his I forget there are other people around.

"Well, you putting your fucking clothes on is pretty high on my list right now," he says, nodding at the dress on the table.

"Why?" I challenge him.

He raises his eyebrows as he leans in and whispers in my ear, "Because seeing you, seeing all this fucking skin, is making my mouth water. I want to bite it, lick it. *Everywhere.* My cock is fucking hard right now, Lily. Because all I can think about is pulling on these little strings, spreading your naked ass on the table, and having dessert. Which is you, by the way. Can you see how that might be an issue for me, considering your family is around?"

My mouth hangs open. *He did not just say that.* I don't even know how to respond. My eyes drift downward, and yep, I can see the outline of one impressive-as-fuck cock, straining against the material of his pants. I reach over, grab the coverall off the table, and put it on.

"Yes! I knew it. You are good," Uncle Zac says,

holding his palm out to my dad, who grunts as he hands my uncle a hundred dollars from his wallet.

"Lily, I thought I taught you to fight better than that," Dad says to me.

"Don't worry, Daddy, it's only the first round," I answer him sweetly, while watching Alex swallow.

"Wait, Lily Pilly, what made you cave so quickly?" Uncle Zac asks.

"Well, I mean, he did just donate one million dollars to the Marine Conservation." I shrug. I'm so not telling him it's because of the impressive boner Alex has.

"Huh. Hey, sunshine?" he calls out to Aunt Lyssa.

"Yeah?" she answers, walking up to the table.

"What charity are you really fond of?" Uncle Zac asks. And I laugh.

"There're heaps, but probably the Children's Cancer Foundation."

"Great. If I donate one million dollars to that foundation right now, would you go and put a top on?" Uncle Zac smiles.

Aunt Lyssa laughs. She's wearing a black halter bikini top with a white sarong wrapped around her waist. "Not a chance, babe. You know I can make that donation myself. I just have to swipe that fancy black card."

"It was worth a shot." He shrugs.

"Dinner's up. Come get it." Uncle Dean, who I've yet to see since I arrived yesterday, sticks his head out the window. I don't know how I've managed to miss him.

I get up and throw my arms around his neck. "Where have you been hiding? And why didn't you take me with you?" I pout at him.

"I just came down. I had shit to do at the house. And if I had known what I know now, I would have taken you with me, darlin', and locked you away in a dungeon somewhere. Maybe with a fucking chastity belt."

"What do you mean? What do you know?" I ask.

"That I'm even more grateful your Aunt Ella gave me a son and not a fucking daughter," he grunts.

"Your loss, Dean. My daughters are fucking awesome! I dare any of you idiots to say otherwise," my dad hollers after him.

And I'm back to wishing the world would swallow me up. I love that my dad's always been my biggest cheerleader, but really. Now? He has to do this now. In front of *him*. I look to Alex, who is watching me with a huge smile on his face.

"Mum, can you please make it stop," I plead. She's the only one who can rein my dad in.

"Well, I could, Lil, but he's not wrong. You two girls *are* fucking awesome." She high-fives my dad.

"Oh my God. I'm going to go get food. Hope?" I look at my sister expectantly.

"Guess I'm getting food too," Hope says.

"Wait for me. I need food too." Breanna comes up

66

the stairs of the deck, with an angry-looking Ash behind her.

"So do I, and a fucking drink," Ash grunts.

I don't wait for them. I walk inside and find Aunt Ella in the kitchen. Her eyes go as wide as saucers when she looks behind me. Glancing over my shoulder, I see I have a shadow in the form of a six-foot brick wall, otherwise known as Alex.

I roll my eyes and head to the food that looks like vegetables. Aunt Ella always keeps the veggies and salads separated from the meats for me. I start loading a plate full of green veggies, potatoes, pumpkin, and salads. It's an odd combo, but I don't care.

"Hi, Alex. I've been hearing *all* about you all night." My aunt holds out a hand to Alex, and he shakes it.

"Hopefully there's been some good things and not all bad."

"A mixture," Aunt Ella admits.

"I'm sure," Alex concedes.

"Oh, here, I found one of Lily and Hope's princess dinner sets. You can give them to Tessie to use."

"Wait, is that Belle? How did I not know you still had this?" I ask, snatching the plate out of Alex's hand.

"Why wouldn't I have them? There are two of them if you want to eat off a princess plate too, Lil." Aunt Ella laughs.

"No, I don't. Here. Sorry," I say to Alex for my rude display. "My aunt needs to be on an episode of *Hoarders*. It's not normal to keep all this shit."

"It's cute." He shrugs. "I still have the first bottle I ever used to feed Tessie."

"That's weird. Maybe we could do like a *Hoarders* neighbours edition." I laugh.

"Don't listen to her, Alex. It's completely normal to have keepsakes. Here, sort yourself out a plate. Vegetarian options on this side, meat-eaters on the other bench over there," Aunt Ella says.

"Thanks. Let me go see what Mia and Tessie want. I'll be right back." He looks down at my plate, his eyebrows creased. But he doesn't say anything.

By the time he comes back inside with Mia and Tessie in tow, my plate is full and I'm walking out to the table. Again, he glares at my dinner like he's scrutinising it. Whatever. I don't care if it looks full. Or if he thinks I shouldn't be eating so much. I mean, it's all veggies and salad. Sure the plate is overfilled, but if you've had my aunt's cooking, your plate would be full too.

I sit down at the almost-empty table. Groaning, I look at my dad, Uncle Zac, and Josh. "Just say it. Get it over with already?" I grit out to them.

"Say what?" Dad asks.

"You know, that I should stay away. That I should not be interested in a guy I know literally nothing about, other than his name's Alex. That you'll make him disappear. I don't know, just say whatever it is you three are going to say."

"I like the guy." Uncle Zac shrugs.

"Honey, you should take your time and get to know him before you do anything else." My dad shakes his head. I laugh at his discomfort. "But I see how he looks at you. He's not going anywhere easily, Lil."

"Not unless I make him disappear. Just say the word, Lily, and I'll do it," Josh suggests. I frown at him.

Pointing my fork in his direction, I threaten, "Do not touch him, Josh."

He holds his hands up in surrender. "Okay, but it's an open offer. Cash it at any time."

Alex sits back down, practically on top of me again. *He's that close.* Tessie and Mia both sit on the opposite side of him.

"Look, Lily. I have a Princess Belle plate. Isn't she pretty?" Tessie says, holding her plate in the air, which Alex bolsters up to prevent the contents from tipping all over the table. His hand literally shot out from nowhere to catch the almost disaster.

"Tessie, she's the best of all the princesses. Do you know why?" I ask her.

"No, why?"

"Because she's smart. She reads so many books and is so smart she saves the Beast from the curse."

"She did save the Beast," Tessie says. "Mummy, can we go to the shops tomorrow?" Tessie turns her attention to Mia.

"Ah, maybe not tomorrow, baby. It's Christmas Eve tomorrow, and it will be way too crowded at the shops."

"But I need more books. I need to be smart like Princess Belle," she complains.

"Hey, Tessie, did you hear that Santa's visiting tomorrow? Maybe you can tell him that you want more books, and he'll bring you some in your stocking," my dad interjects. He's a sucker for a pouting child.

"Ah, maybe... We don't get everything on our list, do we, Tessie? Because Santa has to give to all the children, not just you," Mia corrects my dad.

"But maybe he will give me more books if I ask. I've been very good this year, haven't I, Uncle Alex?" Tessie looks at Alex expectantly.

"You're always good, *bella*. How about you ask Santa tomorrow, and we will see what happens," he replies.

"Yay, I'm getting more books!" Tessie squeals.

"I need grandchildren already. Ash, when are you going to bring me home a baby?" Aunt Lyssa prompts, while smiling at Tessie's excitement.

Both Ash and Breanna almost choke to death. *Well, now that's interesting.*

8

Alex

I can feel the tension amongst the sudden silence. All eyes are on Ash and Breanna. All but mine. No, I'm watching Joshua McKinley. Always keep your eyes on the most dangerous thing in the room. And right now, he looks downright murderous.

I pick up my phone. "Tessie, Uncle Leo wants to

know if he can eat the last of the chocolate ice cream," I say while glancing towards Mia.

She knows the drill. She knows when we tell Tessie this, it means she needs to get herself and my niece out of here and somewhere safe. Tessie, of course, reacts how I expect her to. She jumps up and runs down the stairs, screaming out to Leo. Mia is quick to follow her.

Fuck, I really want to get Lily away from this table too. Leaning into her ear, I whisper, "Lily, can you help me get a glass of water from the kitchen?"

She looks at me, confused, and shakes her head before she goes back to staring at her cousin and Breanna. I watch Emily reach out and grab hold of Josh's hand; the guy looks like he's physically shaking with rage.

"Someone better start fucking talking!" Josh directs his glare towards Ash. "What the fuck did you do?"

Ash stands, and Breanna follows suit. "First, you don't speak to her like that. Second, I don't have to tell you shit. Until you start acting like a human, instead of a fucking rabid dog."

Oh shit, wrong move, bro. I think… It happens so fast. Josh pulls a Glock out from God knows where and aims it right at Ash's head.

Ash moves quickly, shoving Breanna behind him. Or at least he attempts to. She ducks and jumps onto the table like a damn ninja monkey. What the hell kind of family is this? I thought mine was crazy. Standing and bringing Lily to her feet, I move her behind me.

Seconds later, the deck is swarmed by men, *my men*, all with guns pointed at Josh. Fuck, I told Leo I wouldn't fuck this up. But I'm not about to sit around and let Josh kill Lily's cousin. Something tells me she wouldn't like that very much.

"Dad, put the gun down. You are not shooting him," Breanna says as she begins to walk across the table. Ash, the fucker who has no sense of survival, reaches out, grabs her, and places her back on the ground.

"Do not step in front of a fucking gun, Bree," he growls.

"Oh please, he's not going to shoot me. You, on the other hand, he very much will," she yells.

"Well, considering I'm not the one pregnant, I can handle being shot," Ash counters.

"Okay, this has gone far enough. Josh, put the fucking gun down," Ella demands.

"Josh, honey, give me the gun," Emily says, holding her hand out.

He looks to his wife before passing her the firearm without a second thought. I breathe a sigh of relief. That is, until the unmistakable sound of a gunshot goes off and that familiar smoky scent fills the air. Men surround me, pulling at me while attempting to persuade me to move.

"Boss, we need to get you out of here," Steve says.

Who the fuck was shot? I look Lily up and down; she's okay. Her face is white, pale.

"Mum, stop!" Breanna yells.

"Put the fucking gun down. *Now*," Zac, Lily's uncle, growls out as he walks around the table, standing between his son and the other end of the barrel.

"You knocked up my daughter? You could have at least had the balls to date her in public, Ash," Emily says in a quiet voice.

Ash, who is now holding his leg, grits out a groan.

"He didn't... he wasn't the one. I'm not..." Breanna starts to explain.

"Bree, stop. It was me, okay. I got her pregnant. And guess what?" he asks everyone. "I'd do it again." He smiles.

"Joshua, get Emily out of here now," Dean orders.

Ash's mum comes running with a first aid kit. "Ash, do not move. You need to be still. Someone call a fucking ambulance."

"I barely scraped him; he'll survive," Emily snarls.

Lyssa glares at her. "You just shot my son. I'd be very quiet right now if I were you."

"He got my daughter pregnant. She's only twenty-two." Emily shrugs, as if that's reason enough to shoot someone.

"Yeah, last I heard, it takes two people to get pregnant," Zac grunts as he walks around the table.

"I'm not bloody pregnant, you idiots," Breanna yells.

"Wait... you're not?" Ash asks her.

"No, and if you listened to me, instead of hearing

one word and going crazy, you would already know that. Also, if I were pregnant, like I thought I might have been, it wouldn't have been Ash's. We've been together for two weeks. Do the bloody math."

I turn, leaving the McKinleys to sort their own bullshit, and hold Lily in my arms. "Lil, are you okay?" She's still a little pale. Quiet. Fuck it! I'm taking her home.

"Steve, make sure no one other than her sister gets through my door," I whisper. I pick Lily up and walk down the steps with her in my arms.

"Wait, where the fuck do you think you're taking her?" Bray asks as I hit the sand.

I turn and glare at him. "Home." He comes down the stairs. Steve goes to step in front of him. But this is Bray fucking Williamson. Before my eyes, he lays out one of my best men with a single hit.

"That really wasn't necessary," I say.

"No, but it felt good." Bray smirks, shaking his hand out. "Lily, are you okay?" he asks her, swiping at the hair along her forehead.

"Yes." Her voice is quiet as she answers him.

"Do you want to go next door, or do you want to go up to your room here? I need to hear it from you, Lily. I don't want to have to hurt someone you like... *unnecessarily.*"

"I'm fine, Dad. Just go make sure Ash and Bree are okay. Don't let Josh and Emily take her away from him, please?"

"Done. This little sleep over, it's PG. I'm assuming you have guest rooms. She's Catholic, you know. Went to a Catholic girls' school and all," Bray dictates to me.

I fight to hold in my laughter. "Ah, sure, whatever you need to hear." There's no way she's going to be anywhere other than my bed.

"Good. Let's stick with that plan then. I might actually be able to sleep tonight," he mumbles as he walks away.

I carry Lily straight upstairs. Mia's sitting on the couch with Tessie, watching some Christmas Hallmark movie. She turns to say something but chooses not to when she sees we have company.

I sit Lily down on the bed. She's quiet, hasn't said anything. I grab a clean shirt from my closet and come back out. She hasn't moved. Kneeling down in front of her, I ask, "Are you really okay, Lily? Do you need anything? Tea? Wine?"

"I'm fine. I've just never seen anyone shot before. I'm sorry... I don't know what kind of voodoo world I woke up in, but my family is not usually like this. We're not crazy," she says. I quirk an eyebrow in disbelief. "Okay, the McKinleys are always that crazy. But the Williamsons, not so much." She tilts her head at me. "I just realised I don't even know your last name."

"Mancini, Alessandro Mancini." I wait for the shock, the look that tells me she's heard of me before. It doesn't come though.

"You're Italian? I mean, obviously, you look like a freaking god. Of course you're Italian," she rambles.

"You think I look like a god?" I smirk.

"Shut up. You know you do."

"Well, I guess this god just found his angel," I say. She bursts out laughing. She laughs so hard her eyes water. "That bad, huh?" I'm not used to talking to girls. *To making conversation.* Usually, I fuck them and that's it. I wouldn't even be able to tell you any of their names.

"That was really lame. Is that the best pick-up line you got? It can't be. Come on, give me another." She laughs.

"I don't have any. I've never had to pick up girls before."

"Yeah, right. There's no way you're a virgin."

"I didn't claim to be. Girls come to me. I don't go to them." I stand, lift her to her feet, and drag her dress over her head. Pulling the string on her bikini top, I let it fall to the ground. I'm momentarily struck by the sheer beauty of her body. She's so fucking gorgeous. Shaking myself out of my thoughts, I pick up my shirt and put it over her head.

"Ah, okay, *so* not where I thought that was heading." She slinks her arms through the sleeves and pulls the material down over her. It's such a shame to see that beauty covered up.

"Yeah, it's a first for me too. I figured you'd be more

comfortable sleeping in a shirt, instead of half-wet bathers."

"You're right. I would be." She smiles as she reaches under the shirt and drags her bikini bottoms down her legs. Fuck me... This isn't good. How the fuck am I meant to not fuck her into the next century, when she's not wearing any panties? I can see her nipples harden under the thin cotton of the shirt. I pull the blanket back, offering her a spot on the bed. "Come on, let's watch a movie."

"A movie? Okay." She climbs into the bed. I get her settled in next to me, her body snuggled up and curled over my chest, as I flick through the channels. It feels right, having her here with me.

"Anything in particular you want to watch?"

"Um, Alex, do you feel that, or is it just me?"

"Feel what?" I ask, confused.

"This, us, whatever is happening here. I think it's big."

"I feel it too. Whatever it is, it *is* big. I don't understand it fully. But my instincts are screaming at me that you are meant to be here. That you are mine. And I always trust my instincts."

"Do you believe in soul mates?" She lifts her head and looks up at me.

"I do now. If you had asked me two days ago, I would have laughed and said it's something only movies and books sell."

"I always believed. I mean, my parents are soul

mates. Their love is the kind books are written about. I grew up knowing that a love like that exists, and wondered if I'd ever find it." She ducks her head down.

"What about now? Do you think you'll find it?"

"I think I might have already," she confesses.

"Lily, if this is the part where you tell me you're seeing someone, you should reconsider," I grit out.

"I'm not seeing anyone. I mean, I've had boyfriends, but they never last."

"Lily..." I lift her chin. "Next time someone asks if you're seeing someone, you tell them *yes*. You tell them you are Alessandro Mancini's girl." I lean down and claim her lips. *Claim her.*

She pulls away. "And when someone asks you, what will your answer be?"

I smile. "I will say that I am the luckiest motherfucker on earth, because I'm taken by Lily Williamson."

"Good answer," she says before she climbs on top of me, bringing her lips back to mine. I get lost in her. I want to pull her into my skin, to make us one. My hands slide up the hem of her shirt and palm the globes of her ass. *Fuck me.* She grinds down on my cock.

"Ah, Lil, we don't have to do this. I'm more than content to just sleep next to you all night." I don't mean a word of that sentence, but I feel like I should at least try to let her know she can stop. I won't like it, but I'll respect her decision.

"Are you kidding me? I've been thinking about this since I saw you through the window." Her hands eagerly go to my shorts, pulling them down and freeing my raging hard-on.

Her tiny palm wraps around my shaft, her fist pumping up and down slowly. "I wanted it to be my hand doing this to you. I wanted to jump through the window and join you in that shower."

"Mmm, I wish you had," I moan as she begins to quicken her pace. "Lily, if we do this, you do know you're going to be mine, right? There is no going back."

"Is that meant to be a threat?"

"No, it's a warning. I won't ever give you up. You are in my veins. At times, I can be possessive. Arrogant. Protective. But what I promise I will always be is yours." Before I finish my sentence, she has my cock lined up with her entrance. She slowly sinks herself down onto me.

"Fuck, Lily. Fuck." Once she's buried to the hilt, I hold her hips still. I need a moment. She feels so fucking amazing. And I feel like a fucking fourteen-year-old losing his V-card again.

"Are you okay?" Lily asks.

"More than okay. I just... you feel really fucking good. Like, fuck, Lily." Her already tight-as-fuck walls clamp down around me. I lose it. Rolling her over so she's beneath me, I pick her legs up, holding her ankles to my shoulders. I don't make sweet passionate love to her like she deserves. No, I fuck her like the caged animal inside me just found his mate.

"Ahh, oh, fuck. Alex. Yes!" she screams. Her body goes rigid. Her eyes roll back into her head as she leaves this earth, finding a euphoria only a great fucking orgasm can offer. I come right along with her. Her pussy contracts with the aftershocks, milking me for everything I've got. I collapse next to her.

"Please tell me we can do that again." She huffs out a breath.

"Day and night, babe. We're never going to stop doing that," I promise her.

9

Lily

I wake, burning up like I'm in a furnace. Why is it so hot in here? Argh, I bet Ava closed the window again. You would think Uncle Dean and Aunt Ella would at least run the aircon. It's the middle of summer.

Throwing the blankets off, I look down and uncover part of the problem. *Fuck*. Last night hits me like a freight train. Did I really tell Alex I thought we were soul mates? I swear this man fries my brain, and I say the stupidest shit. *Even if I do believe it, did I really have to say it?*

Carefully sliding out from under his arm, I roll off the bed. This isn't my first taste of a shame-driven escape. Not that there's any shame in what that man did to my body last night. No, the shame is over how I practically told him we were soul mates and destined for something big.

I'm not sure why he hasn't called in the doctors and had me committed. I make it to the bedroom door before I hear a deep throat clear behind me. *Shit. Fuckery.* He was not meant to wake up. Turning around, I try to give my sweetest, most confident smile. "Light sleeper?"

"Like you wouldn't believe." He tilts his head. "If you think you're getting out of this room, dressed in only a shirt, think again, Lily."

Damn it! Why does he have to say my name? It just rolls off his tongue and curls around my insides. But to hell if he thinks I'm listening to any man tell me how to dress. I might have caved last night, but it's a new day. And I will not let the Alex fog invade my mind or my free will today.

I look down at the shirt. Remembering my discarded bikini on the floor, I pick it up. It's still damp; the fabric's cold as hell. But I'll be damned if I'm not going to show him a thing or two about who he thinks he's ordering around here.

Pulling the t-shirt up over my head, I throw it on the bed. I bend down, way further than I need to, and drag my bikini bottoms up my legs, wiggling my hips to get them into place. Next, I throw my hair over my shoulder and tie the top on, unnecessarily cupping my breasts in my hands as I adjust the fabric.

I hear the groans coming from the bed. Looking up, I see the sheet tented. Damn it... That looks like an inviting tent to shelter myself in. But no... I am Lily freaking Williamson. I am strong, independent, and I have free will.

"Well, thanks for last night. I guess I'll see you around?" A lot was said between us. But knowing my luck, he probably doles out that sweet shit to all the girls he fucks.

"Lily?" he asks as he gets out of bed. Naked, completely fucking naked. I think I physically drool. Cue the brain fog.

"Ah, yeah?" I try to bring my eyes up to meet his, but there's only so much willpower a girl can have. And his abs and lower body area are just begging to be admired. I mean, it's pointing right at me. It would be rude not to look, right?

Alex lifts my chin, tilting my head upward. "Where are you planning on going?"

"Home. It's Christmas Eve. I have to bake some treats and deliver them to my gran and pops. Then I have to help my mum and aunts prepare whatever it is they're planning on serving tonight. I have to do some last-minute gift shopping too."

"Okay, how about we start with breakfast—*and coffee*. Definitely fucking coffee." He picks me up. My legs automatically wrap around his waist; my whole body is betraying me right now. I need to leave, not further entangle myself with Alex.

He walks into an impressive-looking wardrobe. My mum would love to get her hands on this wardrobe. He sets me on the island bench, and I watch as he puts a pair of loose-fitting black shorts on. He picks up a shirt, and I almost whine at the thought of him covered up. But then he pulls the shirt over my head.

My arms, having a mind of their own, find themselves through the sleeves—much like last night. Damn it! He's done it again. I had every intention of storming out of this house in a bikini and telling him where he could shove his shirt.

"Come on, let's get you fed. You didn't eat much last night. You must be starving."

I follow Alex downstairs, my hand firmly clasped in his as he leads me through his house. I wouldn't need to follow him though. I've been in this house just as much as my aunt's house next door. The Fosters used to own it. They had three daughters and one boy. Hope and I used to joke that they were our holiday friends. Every holiday we spent at my aunt's, they would be there. We used to get into all sorts of mischief together.

What I loved most about playing in this house, though, were the hidden rooms. I wonder if Alex knows they exist yet? He probably does. There are so many memories. My and Hope's first kisses were in this house, when we played spin the bottle with Shaun Foster. *He was cute.* At fourteen, neither of us had kissed anyone yet.

One of Shaun's friends dared us both to kiss Shaun. Not at the same time. I made Hope go first; she really liked him. She'd go on and on about it. Their kiss was a proper kiss, full of tongue and all. When it was my turn, I gave him the quickest peck on the lips I could. It was gross.

Everyone laughed, except Hope. All the boys said I was frigid. My sister and I took one look at each other as they all continued to snicker at my expense. By the time we left that house, they never dared tease us again. You don't grow up with your parents owning a string of MMA gyms without learning a thing or two.

My dad made sure Hope and I could fight and defend ourselves. It was important to him that we weren't helpless girls who needed a man to protect us. *His words, not mine.* Even though he wanted us to know how to fight, we both got grounded for two weeks after we dropped those boys on their asses.

If we had told Dad why we did it, instead of being so bloody stubborn and keeping that secret, he probably would have rewarded us rather than ground us. I chuckle at the thought.

Alex pivots to face me. "Something amusing?"

"Not really, just a memory of when Hope and I were kids." I expect him to turn back around and start walking, but he doesn't. He just stares at me, waiting, like he wants me to elaborate further. Let's see how much he actually wants to hear.

"Hope and I used to hang around with the kids that lived here when we were young. The Fosters owned this home. Anyway, they had a son. Shaun, he was hot. *Like really hot.*" I waggle my eyebrows for good measure. "One day, when we were fourteen, we played spin the bottle with Shaun and his friends. Anyway, long story short, I had my very first kiss in this house."

Alex's jaw tightens. He doesn't say anything as he turns and continues walking towards the kitchen. When we enter, there's a man making coffee. I can hear a television coming from somewhere, playing cartoons. Turning around, I see through a doorway into a dining room. Tessie and Mia are seated at a table. There's a television on the wall. Tessie is eating pancakes as she watches cartoons.

Alex leads me over to the bench. "How do you have your coffee?" His voice is gruff, and the tone is one I haven't heard him use before.

The man at the bench drops a spoon loudly into the sink. Without saying a word, he looks between Alex and me. *Watching.*

"Ah, almond milk, no sugar. But you know, I can go

back to my aunt's. Uncle Zac does make really good coffee." I motion to stand.

"Sit down. Trust me, mine's better," he grumbles. Something tells me he's not referring to coffee.

"Okay then." I stay seated.

"Leo, get me a new real estate agent. Not the same idiot as last time. We're selling this fucking house." Alex presses buttons on an impressive-looking coffee machine. He goes to the fridge and stares at the contents, like he's waiting for something to appear. "Fuck." He closes the door, pulls his phone out, and taps away. Moments later, his phone pings—I'm assuming with a response.

"Why exactly are you selling a house you just bought?" Leo asks.

"I suddenly don't like it as much," Alex answers while looking at me.

"Maybe Hope and I can buy it from you then. It does hold such fond memories for us," I suggest.

Alex smirks at me. "Really? Fond memories, Lily? One of them being the first time you kissed a boy at the extremely young age of fourteen?"

"Yep, among others." I nod.

"You what?" Oh crap, I cringe at the sound of my dad's voice booming from behind me. Spinning around, I use the sweetest tone I can muster before I've had my morning coffee.

"Dad? What are you doing here?"

"Being the milkman apparently?" He places a carton of almond milk on the bench.

"Hold up. Mr. Williamson, can I just say it's an honour to meet you. I'm Leo. Also, one of your biggest fucking fans." Leo holds out a palm and shakes my dad's hand.

"Thanks, I think," my dad answers.

"Oh, man. Alex, you know who this is, right? Bray fucking Williamson. The guy's a legend." Leo is fangirling over my dad. It's weird. I know my dad was huge in the underground MMA scene before Hope and I were born. But Leo doesn't look old enough to have been around back then.

"So, Lily, the Foster boy? Really? I never did like that fucking kid." My first kiss is not something I ever needed to talk to my dad about.

"Well, Hope did it first, and she used tongue and all. I only pecked him. Very quickly, mind you. Remember that time you grounded us for beating them up?".

"Yes."

"Wait, you beat up boys?" Leo asks me. I look to Alex, who is just watching, observing this whole conversation he willingly subjected me to. He knew my dad was behind me. *The ass.*

"Yep, didn't stop until they cried," I say proudly. "I can give you a demonstration if you'd like?" I offer.

"Either of you take her up on that, I'll drop you before you ever get near her," my dad warns them.

Leo holds his hands up. "Wouldn't dream of it. Besides, if I did, I'd have to let you win, Lily. I don't fancy being stuck at the bottom of the Sydney Harbour for eternity."

"What?"

"No one is fucking fighting you, Lily. Here, try this." Alex puts a steaming cup of coffee in front of me. I take a sip, releasing an involuntary moan. "This is good, like I'd marry you just to wake up to this coffee every day good," I blurt out.

"Leo, forget the agent. Get a jeweller here," Alex demands. I choke on the coffee I was about to swallow.

My dad slaps me on the back. "Breathe, Lily."

"I was joking, Alex. Leo, do not get a jeweller out here," I squeak.

"Sorry, Lily, I gotta do what the boss says. So, what kind of cut are we talking? Princess, oval, square?" Leo asks me.

"None of the above," I answer.

My dad laughs next to me. I glare at him. Why is he laughing? This is not funny. "Why aren't you disposing of his body right now? He thinks he's going to marry me." I don't understand this sudden turnaround from my dad.

"I like him. Alex, you have my blessing. Not that you bothered to ask for it," my dad says.

"I wouldn't ask. She's not a piece of property for you to sign over. When I ask her to marry me, that choice is hers and hers alone." Okay, well, that was a really good answer. I try not to swoon.

"And if I say no?" I ask him.

"I'll keep asking until you say yes. Come on, let's eat. Bray, you're welcome to stay for breakfast?"

"No, I'm good. I'm about to go and ground Hope again. The fucking Foster kid..." My dad shakes his head as he leaves.

"Okay, what did you do to my dad? And why the hell does he like you so much?"

"No idea. But whatever it is, let's keep it that way. It makes life so much easier if your family isn't fighting me." He walks up to me, spreads my legs, and steps between them. Leo makes himself scarce, heading into the dining room. "I'm keeping you, Lily. No matter what anyone says." His lips descend onto mine.

"Mmm, don't you think this is all too fast? You just met me yesterday, and you're talking about marriage. It's crazy."

"It's fast. But I feel it in my gut. It's also right. If I fired up a jet right now and took you to Vegas, would you say no?"

"It depends."

"On what?"

"Two things. Would that jet be big enough to take my whole family with me? And how quickly can I get a script for Xanax filled?"

"Okay. For your whole family, we'd probably need more than one jet. That can be arranged. As for the

Xanax? You do know I'm Alessandro Mancini, right? I can get you anything you desire, Lily. At the click of a finger, I can have whatever it is you want at that door. But why Xanax?"

"What does that mean? Alessandro Mancini? Are you like *the Godfather* or something? A mobster. Are you famous? Should I know who you are? Also, I may have a little fear of flying. So, yes, I need Xanax to get on a jet."

"Ah, we can come back to this conversation. All you need to know right now, no matter what you might hear about me, is that I won't let any of my world touch you." He cups my face and kisses the hell out of me, and just like that I forget the million questions I had.

10

Alex

After breakfast, Lily went back to her aunt's to bake. I tried to follow her. She didn't really like that, said something about me distracting her and burnt cookies. It's been exactly three hours since she left, and I'm sitting around here pining like a lost fucking puppy.

I took my frustrations out on the fucking asshole who thought he'd take pictures of me and Lily in the ocean last night. Let's just say… he won't be making that mistake again. Unfortunately, the cocksucker had already sent the pictures to an email address. Leo is working on finding out who the fuck that address belongs to. And more importantly, why they're so interested in receiving pictures of me.

I'm getting antsy about Lily being next door without me for so long. What if whoever wanted those pictures figures out who she is? I had Steve arrange for an additional ten men to come out here. It's Christmas; they should be at home, celebrating with their fucking families. None of them complained though. I'm sure the Christmas bonuses they receive keep them plenty happy.

I pay my men accordingly. If you pay them too little, they'll be tempted to sell you out to the highest bidder. Pay them too much, and they'll begin to think they've got bigger dicks than you do. It'll start a pissing match—one that often leads to them attempting to take what you have. I've dealt with my fair share of rats and traitors over the years. It never ends well for them.

"Boss." Leo knocks on my office door. "The jeweller is here. Want me to send him in?"

"Yes," I answer.

"Sure, ah, Alex, are you really sure about this? I mean, you just met the girl yesterday? Don't you wanna… I don't know… wait a little longer?"

"It's fucking crazy, but I feel it right down to my bones. Lily is meant to be mine, Leo."

"Okay, it's your funeral." He shrugs and walks out the door, returning with an older-looking man, carrying a case and closely followed by his own security.

"Mr. Raffe, thank you for coming on such short notice." I stand, shaking his hand.

"Of course, Mr. Mancini. I've brought a range of items for you to peruse. See if anything is special enough for what you have in mind." He opens his case and I spot it right away. I point to a ring off to the side; it's in the shape of a lily flower. It has a princess-cut diamond in the middle with smaller diamonds encrusted on what looks to be petals. It's fucking perfect. "Ah, the lily. Great choice. This is a three-carat stone, with a further two carats in weight surrounding it."

"I'll take it." I'm about to turn away when a pair of earrings catches my eye. "Those too. Leo will process the funds for you. If you'll excuse me, I've got somewhere I need to be."

Walking out of the room, I head next door. It's been three fucking hours. I'm sure it doesn't take this long to bake cookies.

Knocking on the door, I'm greeted by Hope. "Wow, three hours. You really went the distance, huh?"

"Three hours? It felt like ten. Where is she, Hope?" I know I'm an asshole.

"How do you know I'm not Lily?" She puts her hands on her hips.

"I just know." I decide it's best to leave out the explanation that my cock doesn't grow hard when I look at her. Her sister though, one glance and I'm ready to fucking go round after round.

"A man of many words. Lily's upstairs, but you can come in. I'll go get her."

"Thank you." I walk inside and head straight for the kitchen bench; there's a tray of brownies set on top. Figuring they're out for the taking, I pick up a piece. A second later, I'm spitting it back out into my hand.

"Yeah, it's safer not to eat those." This comes from Zac.

"What is it? I thought it was a brownie." I walk around the bench, find a bin, and head to the sink to wash my hands.

"*That* would be Lily's vegan version of a brownie."

He laughs. "You should probably get used to them. That girl loves to bake."

"And no one's told her that maybe she shouldn't?" I inquire.

"By all means, feel free to tell her." He laughs. "Just make sure I'm around to see it."

"Tell me what?" Lily comes into the kitchen, and all of the air leaves my lungs. She's so goddamn beautiful it fucking hurts.

"That your little boyfriend here stole one of your brownies." Zac wraps his arm around her shoulder. Even knowing he's her uncle, I want to rip his fucking arm off her. It's irrational, I know.

"Oh, did you like it, Alex? What did you think? Do you want another one?" Lily asks excitedly.

I can't bring myself to tell her it's complete shit and tastes like cardboard. She's so fucking cute with how excited she is that I ate one of her brownies. "Loved it, Lily. I'm sure anything you make is amazing. But didn't you make these to take to your gran and pops?"

"I did, but here, have another one. They won't eat that many anyway."

I take the proffered brownie. "Thanks." I plaster a smile on my face. *I can do this.* I've stomached much worse than a vegan-fucking-imitation brownie. Biting into it, I block out the burnt cardboard taste and moan. "What do you do with these?"

"It's a secret. Do you want me to make you your own batch to take home?" At this, Zac coughs into his hand.

"I think I hear Aunt Lyssa calling. Lily, your boyfriend's never invited to poker night," he says, walking out.

"Don't worry, poker nights are boring as shit. Ash and Breanna always win anyway," Lily says as she looks me up and down. "Why are you all dressed up? Don't get me wrong, it's a good look on you, but why?"

"I was working."

"On Christmas Eve? At the beach?"

"Work never stops when you're at the top."

"Do you always dress like you've just stepped out of a magazine when you're working?"

"Do I always wear a suit? Yes," I answer, picking at a piece of imaginary fluff on my jacket.

"Alex, it's thirty-five degrees outside. Layman's terms: that's hot as fuck."

"I'm used to it. "

"Morning, Alex. Wait, how the hell did you get that?" Lily's mum asks as she stops in front of me.

"Ah, get what?"

"That suit; it's Armani's fall collection. It's not even available here yet." Her hands come up to the lapels of my jacket and run along the fabric. I look to Lily, with my palms in the air.

"Ah, Lily, a little help here." She rolls her eyes at me.

"Dad, Mum's feeling up Alex. You might want to get out here before she jumps ship," Lily calls out.

My eyes go wide. Great, the last thing I need is her

dad thinking I've got the hots for his fucking wife. "Not helpful, Lily."

"No, but it's funny."

"Well, he's very attractive, Lily. You could do worse," her mum says as she heads to the fridge.

"Rye, why are you feeling up our daughter's boyfriend?" Bray storms into the kitchen, a scowl on his face.

"First, not my boyfriend. And second, it was more his clothes she was feeling than him, really," Lily answers. I screw my face up at her. Not her boyfriend? *Yeah, right.* This is something we need to discuss, just not in front of her parents.

"Why are you in my kitchen, wearing a suit?" Bray asks me.

"I was working. Came to offer Lily a lift to wherever it is she needs to go today."

"You do know it's Christmas Eve, and hot as fuck out," Bray says.

"That's what I said, Dad," Lily pipes in.

I unbutton my jacket, take it off, and throw it over one of the bar stools. Removing my cufflinks, I fold the sleeves of my white dress shirt, then loosen and remove my tie.

"Better?" I ask them all, considering they're overly invested in my attire.

"Not at all. Now I just want to..." Lily stops and covers her mouth.

"I'm so glad you fucking didn't finish that sentence, Lil," Bray says.

"She wants to climb you like a monkey and do very unspeakable things to you," Hope announces as she walks into the room.

"Reilly, make it stop. Make them stop." Bray covers his ears.

Reilly goes up to him and not-so-quietly says, "Come on, babe, I want to do some very unspeakable things to you." They leave the kitchen so fast it's almost comical. I can see what Lily meant by watching her parents' love and hoping to find something just like that.

"Ah, well, it's nice of you to offer to take me today. But Hope and I usually go together. And there's a list of things I need to do. So, you should probably just... I don't know... do what it is you do. And maybe I'll see you tonight?" Lily starts packing the brownies into a container.

"It's a good thing my car can fit more than two people. I'll take you both. What is it you have to do?"

"Well, go to Gran and Pop's. Then I've gotta hit the shops. There's some last-minute shopping I need to do. Then come back. Santa is making an appearance for the first time in years, so that is not something we are missing." Lily points between herself and her twin.

"Your family's having another get-together tonight? Is that wise?"

"It's Christmas Eve. Of course. Besides, Ash is fine.

He's a dumbass for admitting to sleeping with Bree in front of her parents. Everyone knows Josh and Emily can be... *unhinged.*"

"Okay, well, as the good twin—she's the evil one," Hope says, pointing to Lily, "I feel like I should warn you. Shopping with her is not an enjoyable experience. It's a nightmare. Your feet will end up one big blister from the amount of stores she drags you through."

"I'm sure I can handle a little shopping," I say, leading them out to the car.

"Lily, I forgot to tell you. This dress, you look fucking gorgeous." I open the car door for her.

"I take it back! This is the worst fucking torture I've ever had to endure. And that's saying a lot," I complain as I slump down into the car. I've just spent four hours, four fucking hours, walking around department store after department store. I mean, they all had the same shit. Why she had to go to all of them, only to end up back at the very first one again, I will never understand.

"Told you so," Hope groans in the back seat.

Even the men I had trailing us started to look like they would rather take a bullet than endure the slow torture.

"I did tell you that you could have stayed home," Lily huffs.

"And miss out on spending the day with you? Never." I wink at her.

"So, who do you think will be forced into the Santa suit this year?" Hope asks.

"It was Dad's great idea, so my guess is him. Although, they might make Josh do it, considering he and Emily went nuts last night. You know, as punishment."

"Joshua McKinley in a Santa suit? I can't see it."

"He was the best Santa when we were kids. We always knew when it was him because he gave the best gifts. One year, his Santa gave us twin ponies. Well, they weren't really twins, but they looked like it and we thought they were. They also came with a deed to a property where we could keep them. We don't have the ponies anymore, but we still have the stables, with horses."

"How old were you?"

"Ten."

"He gave you a deed to a property when you were ten? That's insane. You know that, right?"

"Yep, but I mean, *ponies*. Matching ponies, Alex. Does Tessie have a pony yet?"

"No, and she's not getting one either. Those things

are messy—*dangerous and messy*." There is no way she's getting a pony. She'd end up falling off it and breaking a bone or something. Lily's tapping away on her phone and smiling. "Lily, do not get her a pony."

"Don't worry, *I* won't get her a pony."

11

Lily

I'll never admit it, but I'm relieved to now have my feet up, sitting outside on my aunt's deck while sipping on a cold glass of Moscato. Everyone's here; there's tension between Aunt Lyssa and Emily. But everyone else seems to have moved past the whole Ash and Bree thing. Well, maybe not Josh. I haven't seen him yet, so I'm assuming he'll be the designated Santa.

The deck is decorated with Christmas lights, and the tree inside my aunt's house is stacked up with a million gifts. I really freaking love Christmas. I sing along to the Christmas carols playing in the background. I'm waiting, not so patiently, for Alex to return. He said he was just ducking home to get Tessie, Mia, and Leo. That was thirty minutes ago. I don't know what's taking him so long. I need to calm the hell down. I'm turning into a stage-five clinger before my own eyes. My mum sits next to me, a glass of wine and a bowl of peanuts in her hands.

"So, Alex, huh?" she says.

"What about him?" I ask nonchalantly.

"You like him, like him. How serious is this? Am I getting grandbabies in the near future? Or is it more of an experimental phase thing?"

"Jeez, Mum, how old are you? Yes, I like him, like him. Grandbabies, *hell no*. And I'm sure there're plenty of experimental things I want to do with that man."

"Okay, well, you know if you happen to give me grandbabies before Ash impregnates Bree, and we all go down in that flame of fire, I'd be really fucking pleased."

"No to the grandbabies still," I say. I have no intention of having kids anytime soon. I have very strong birth control methods.

"You know, you and Hope were the best things your dad and I ever made." *Oh great, here comes the "wistful reflecting on the past" part of the night.* "I wish we could turn back time and you'd be little again. Christmas is always so much more fun with kids around."

"I'm still your kid, mum. Feel free to spoil me rotten with gifts." I laugh at her frown.

"That's not the point. Where is this boyfriend of yours anyway?"

"He went to get his sister and Tessie." I look over to his house. There is no sign of movement at all. "Maybe I should go over and see if they need help?" I suggest. As I do, Tessie comes running up the beach with Mia, Alex, and Leo right behind her.

"Lily, Lily!" She stops in front of me, huffing and puffing. "Are you Lily or Hope?"

"Lily."

"Phew, has Santa been here yet? Did I miss him?"

"Nope, I think you're right on time." I point down the beach, where a grumpy-looking Santa is leading a pony up to the house. Alex groans at the sight.

Tessie jumps up and down on the spot. "Mummy, it's really Santa. He's here."

"I know. How exciting." Mia smiles.

"Ho-ho-ho. I've been told there is a little girl here who's been good all year? Who could it be?" Josh, AKA Santa, looks around at all of us, then down to Tessie. "It must be you. You look like the best girl here." He winks.

"It *is* me! I've been very good, Santa." She jumps up and runs towards him. Alex stops her by scooping her at the waist and picking her up.

"Tessie, you can't run at Santa. He has a pony. We don't know if it bites."

"Ponies don't bite, Uncle Alex," she says seriously.

"I heard you didn't have a pony of your own, Tessie, so this one is just for you. To keep," Santa tells her.

"I get a pony? A real-life pony? Can I name her?"

"You sure can. Want to go for a ride?" Santa asks.

"No, she doesn't. Is that even safe? What if it kicks or takes off running or bites?" Alex says.

"Oh my God, Alex. One time. You got bitten one time. Get over it. Come on, sweetie, let's go look at the pony." Mia takes Tessie from Alex.

"Mia, at least put a helmet on her," he calls out after them. "Leo, follow them. Make sure she doesn't fall." Leo walks behind them as Santa takes Tessie around the beach on the pony.

"You know ponies are safe. Even if she did fall, it's not like it's high." I laugh.

"I thought I specifically requested you didn't get her a pony, Lily. Do you know how messy those things are?" he complains as he sits next to me and kisses my forehead. The gesture is at odds with his sour mood.

"I do, actually. And she can keep it at my stables. It's fine. Also, I didn't buy her the pony. Josh did."

"Josh... why?"

"I told him she didn't have one. Josh is a sucker for gifts, always wants to give the biggest and best."

We've all just sat down to dinner. I notice Alex doesn't have any meat on his plate again. He's copied my plate full of veggies. "Are you vegan? Or vegetarian?" I ask him. Mia hears the question and laughs.

"No," he answers.

"Well, why don't you eat the meat or seafood?"

He leans into me. "I very much intend on finding some mistletoe and kissing the shit out of you. I'd prefer not to taste like something you don't like when I do."

"Oh, okay." I look from side to side. Surely Aunt Ella has mistletoe somewhere around here. "Aunt Ella, where's the closest mistletoe?" I ask across the table. My dad groans and glares at me and Alex.

"There isn't any. Mum took it and threw it all away that year she caught me making out with Sally under the stairs," Dominic complains.

"Sally from next door? Fuck, I'm glad the Fosters sold that house," my dad mumbles.

"Remember the little secret rooms we'd play hide and seek in?" Hope asks.

"Yep, that house was fucking awesome. I heard

you're looking to sell it, Alex. Maybe I should buy it," Ash offers.

"He's not selling it to you. Hope and I are buying it."

"I think I'd rather see it burned," Alex grunts.

"Well, looks like you're not the only one." Bree points towards Alex's house, where there is currently a heap of smoke billowing out from the windows.

"Fuck." Alex jumps up. He starts towards the house, then stops. "Mia, sugar!" he yells. Mia quickly grabs Tessie, throwing her under the table. Alex turns to the rest of us. "You all need to get down. Right the fuck now." He picks me up and tosses me to the ground, landing on top of me. His hands cover my ears as the loudest mixture of noises pierces through them. It's an odd sound, like a continuous popping, competing with a series of whistles and crashing.

I try to raise my head. *Where the hell is Hope? Mum and Dad?* Alex lifts his body off mine, bringing me to my feet. His hands run over every inch of me, as do his eyes. "Are you okay? Are you hurt anywhere?"

"I'm fine. Where's my sister?" I look around and see Hope sitting on the ground, my mum and dad crouching in front of her.

"Lily, she's okay. Your parents are with her." Alex tries to calm me down. She's not okay though. I know my sister. And she's fragile. No one, other than my parents, knows just how much so.

"No, she's not." I head over to Hope, sitting next to

her, and she collapses into my arms. "Shh, it's okay. I'm here. It's going to be okay, Hope. I promise." I glance up at Alex's face. He's watching me with an indecipherable look in his eyes. I pray that my words of comfort are true. "It's okay, Hope," I whisper to her, over and over again.

"We need to get her out of here," my dad says.

"I'll have cars waiting out front in ten minutes, Lil. We need to go," Alex states. My dad lifts Hope into his arms and carries her through the house.

"Go where?" I ask Alex. Mia and a crying Tessie walk past with Leo right behind them.

"I have a property, not far from here. Let's go there for now."

Josh comes up next to me. "Is there a reason someone just blew up your house?"

"Probably."

"Do you know who?" Josh looks pissed. I step in front of Alex. I know how unpredictable Josh is, but I also know he's not ever going to hurt me.

"Josh, this isn't Alex's fault. It was probably an accident. I was baking in his kitchen. I probably left the oven on or something. You know how forgetful I can be."

Josh laughs. "Sure, whatever you say, Lil. I want a name, Alex." He follows us inside. Everyone seems to be leaving through the house. The deck is full of men in suits—men surrounding Alex and me.

"Lily, you don't need to lie for me. I can handle Josh." Alex smiles, wrapping an arm around me.

"You don't know how crazy he can be, Alex."

"I assure you, Lily, I'm worse." He winks.

After about half an hour of arguments between everyone, we finally all agreed to come to Alex's house. Most of the family wanted to go to the McKinley Estate. I didn't want to leave Alex, but I also didn't want to miss seeing my family on Christmas. My mum and dad realized how torn up I was over the situation and said they were going with me. If everyone else didn't tag along, that was their choice. The thing with my family though... they're a super tight-knit bunch. And Christmas is extra special for my Uncle Zac. He's always made sure everyone is together every year.

So, after thirty minutes of arguing, and about a fifteen-minute drive, we finally made it to Alex's other house. When Alex said he had another property, I wasn't exactly expecting *this*. This place puts Uncle Dean and Aunt Ella's home to shame, and theirs is a freaking museum. I look around and notice there're no Christmas trees, no decorations, no lights—nothing.

"What's wrong?" Alex doesn't miss much.

"Nothing, I just... I need to make sure Hope is okay."

The way Alex is looking at me tells me he doesn't believe me. He's searching my eyes for another tell. After a minute, he says, "Okay, I'll have someone bring her in something. She's in the room just down that hall, third door on your right." He leans in and kisses my forehead. It's something my dad and uncles have always done, but when Alex does it, that touch of his lips on my skin sends fiery heat throughout my body.

"Thank you." I practically run down the hall. Opening the door, I find Hope sitting with her back against the head of the bed; she's between my mum and dad. "Hope, are you okay?" She nods.

"Come on, Lil, get in." My dad moves over and I sit next to him and Hope. "Are you okay?" he asks me.

"Yeah, I'm fine."

"Lily, this guy... Alex. How deep are you into this already?" my dad prompts.

"Pretty deep. It's stupid, I know. It's been two days. I barely know him, yet I do. Does that make sense?"

"It does." He wraps an arm around me. "I just want you girls to be happy. And safe. I'm sure you'll be happy with him, but will you be safe?" he whispers.

"I don't know," I answer truthfully.

"Don't be stupid. You can see that boy would take a

bullet for her. Have you seen the way he watches her? It's borderline obsessive," my mum adds.

"Oh, like how Dad looks at you?" Hope interjects.

"Yeah, like that," Mum responds wistfully.

"What are we going to do about Christmas?" I ask. I know it's a stupid thing to focus on right now. I mean, Alex's house just blew up. "Oh my gosh, Tessie probably has no gifts. They would have been in that house..."

"I'll sort it out. Don't worry." My dad gets up. As he exits the room, a maid comes in with a trolley of hot drinks and food.

I wait for the woman to leave before I turn back to Hope. "Are you sure you're okay?"

"I'm fine, Lil, promise. The blast just shocked me a little. I'll be fine. I had a momentary panic attack—that's all it was."

"Okay." I drop the subject, although I know she's anything but okay. "Now, can we talk about me and how freaking hot Alex is?" I laugh.

"He does dress really great. And on that note, I'm out of here. I'll be just outside if you need me, baby," Mum says to Hope.

"Okay, so what are we talking? *This*, or this?" Hope moves her hands in a bigger or smaller gesture.

Adjusting her outstretched arms to the approximate size, I tell her, "This." Her mouth goes wide.

"No way. That's impossible. How does that even fit?" She screws her face up.

"No idea, but it did, and so bloody good too."

By the time Alex knocks on the door, I've spent an hour chatting about everything I can think of. It's a way to help keep her mind from going backwards. "Can I come in?" he asks.

"Sure, it is your house," Hope answers for me.

Alex sits on the bed, right next to me, before reaching for my hand. "Lily, your dad wanted to ask you something. I forget what it was, but he's in the foyer, taking the house over."

"Ah, okay. I'll be right back then?" I question. I look to Hope to make sure she's okay with me leaving her in here with Alex. We don't need to communicate verbally; we each just know what the other is thinking.

"I'll wait here," Alex says with a groan as I climb over him to get out of the bed.

12

Alex

When I saw the fire billowing out of the beach house, I knew it was no accident. Someone actually blew up my fucking house. My family could have been in that house. In the few hours that have passed, Leo, Josh, and I have surprisingly worked together, digging through every bit of security footage we could hack into from the neighbouring properties. It didn't take long to identify the culprits.

It wasn't an easy thing, to let Josh assist with this. But the fucking psycho wouldn't take no for an answer. Then he told me he could work with me *or alone.* But someone put his family in danger, and he'd find them before I did. I wasn't prepared to risk him getting his hands on them first. That attack was directed at me and mine. I want to know who the fuck is behind it. I want to rip their fucking hearts out of their chests.

Leo and a few of the men are out on the streets now, hunting down the two guys who were caught on the CCTV entering and leaving the property. I'm guessing the merger I was working on with McKinley Industries is out the fucking window now. That's not going to be a pleasant fucking conversation with the investors. Unfortunately, I can't handle my legitimate businesses the same way I handle the others. The two don't tend to cross.

All I wanted was a nice, quiet beach Christmas for Tessie. But I've ended up with a fucking huge-as-fuck extended family, which came attached to Lily, and some fucker who is hell-bent on destroying me. Like the others before them, they can try, but I guarantee they won't fucking succeed.

I need to get back to Lily. Entering the living room, I realize it suddenly looks like a freaking circus. Lily's parents, along with her aunts and uncles, are all directing people carrying what looks like Christmas shit through the house.

"What's going on?" I ask Dean.

"It's Christmas, mate. You can't wake up on Christmas morning and not have decorations." I raise my eyebrows at him. "Don't stress. We'll have it sorted in no time. This house of yours is going to look like Christmas threw up all over it." He follows Ella, who's struggling with a box.

"Great, perfect. A house covered in Christmas vomit. What could be better?" I mumble.

"Please, for the love of God, tell me you're not a grinch. I can look past a lot of shit for my daughter's happiness. But a grinch? That's a deal breaker." Bray steps in front of me, arms folded over his chest.

"You're actually serious?" I ask, shocked.

"Fucking oath, I am."

"I'm not a grinch. Tired as fuck, but a grinch? No. I just bought a four-million-dollar house so my five-year-old niece could have her dream beach Christmas. Does that sound like a grinch to you?"

"Oh, thank fuck. You had me worried there for a minute. We don't accept any grinches into the family. It's a thing," he says.

"It's not a thing. It's *his* thing," Zac interjects. "Where do you want the tree?"

I really don't fucking care, but I feel like that's probably not the right answer. "Ah, check with Lily—wherever she wants it," I say as I make a quick escape.

I find Lily and Hope in the bedroom. Sitting down next to them, I tell Lily her dad wants her. Really, I wanted to talk to Hope. Also, I don't want to deal with the chaos that's outside this room right now.

"Are you good?" I ask Hope.

"Yes, thank you," she says quietly.

"Want to talk about it?"

"Do you ever feel like something that happened a long time ago just won't ever leave you? Like no matter how hard you try, you can't escape it?"

"I did once." I think about the childhood Mia and I had. It was rough. I used to let it dictate a lot of the things I did, along with the anger and hatred I carried inside me.

"What changed? How did you fix it?"

"I accepted that it wasn't my fault, that things happened beyond my control. I stopped trying to escape the memories and just let them be." I'm not sure I'm explaining it right...

"I don't know if I'm ready for that," she says.

"Well, in the meantime, if you need me to help with anything, I'll be here. I'm sorry about what happened tonight."

"Why are you being nice to me? You know she's already smitten, right? You don't need to win over the sister." Hope laughs.

"You're a big part of Lily. And she's a big part of me, it seems, which makes you very important to me, Hope. I mean it, if you ever need anything—doesn't matter how crazy it is—I'll find a way to help you. Also,

I don't want to be out there. Your family is a little Christmas nuts."

"Wait until morning. That's when you'll see the real crazy come out. You should be warned not to sleep naked tonight."

"What the hell, Hope? I leave you alone for five minutes, and you're talking about him being naked? Seriously, if you weren't like the literal other half of me, I'd cut a bitch." Lily laughs as she jumps on the bed and wrestles Hope. They're both laughing, so I'm assuming they're not actually fighting.

But fuck, these girls have some impressive moves. Hope somehow manages to roll out, and she flips Lily over, landing on top of her. Hope has her pinned down. I'm about to jump in and pull Hope off when Lily glares at me. "Don't you dare. Stay right where you are."

I hold my hands up. "Why do I feel like I need to go get your mum to come separate you two right now?" I laugh. Lily brings her legs up, in some kind of flexible ninja move, and flips Hope again. They both land on the floor, taking the bedside lamp with them. They don't stop though; they continue rolling around. "I swear to fucking God, Lily, if you cut yourself on that broken glass, I'm gonna be pissed."

"Well, if she tapped out, I could stop."

"Never going to happen," Hope giggles.

"What the hell is going on?" Bray walks through the door, closely followed by Zac and Dean.

"Fifty on Hope," Zac says.

"No way. It's Lily's turn for a win. I'm going in with a thousand on Lil. Don't give up, Lil. You can do this," Dean hollers.

Bray steps over both girls towards me. "You grab Lily. I'll grab Hope. If we don't stop them, we will be here all night, until they finally tire out. They're both too fucking stubborn to tap out." He doesn't wait for me to respond; he bends down and starts pulling the girls apart.

I guess I am going to have to be brave and grab Lily then. "Sorry, Lily, it's late. Maybe you can continue this another day," I suggest as I pull her up and hold her body tight against mine. If I thought she'd go easy on me, I found out I was wrong—the hard way—when she fucking flips me onto my back. *Literally fucking flips me.* I was standing there one minute and on the floor on my back the next, with Lily leaning over me.

"Huh, perfect form, Lil," Bray says proudly.

"What the fuck? What did I do?" I ask.

"Nothing, but I kinda always wanted to try that on someone who wasn't a gym partner. It actually works." She beams. It's hard to be pissed when she sends me that smile. I'd let her flip me a million times over if I got that smile in return.

I stand up and dust myself off. "Well, it's been an eventful night. If you'll excuse us, we will see you all in the morning." Bending my shoulder to Lily's waist, I pick her up and walk out. "Huh, what'd you know. That move works too." I laugh.

"Alex, not funny. Put me down." She hits my back.

"No, I don't think I will."

"Everyone can see up my dress, you know." She's back on her feet in seconds. I straighten her clothes, pulling the hemline as far down as I can. I lead her up the stairs and into the master suite—straight through to the shower. I need to get her naked, sooner rather than later.

13

Lily

*A*lex turns the shower on, testing the water. And all I can think is: *Yes! I'm finally getting in the shower with the man from the window.* I should probably be demure or some shit and follow his lead. But I'm so not that girl. I know I'm coming back into this bathroom later to appreciate the beauty of it, like it deserves. But right now, the only thing I'm appreciating is the beauty of the man right in front of me.

I make extra quick work of stripping my clothes off. By the time Alex turns back to me, satisfied with the temperature of the water, I'm standing before him completely naked.

Alex's eyes go wide as they rake up and down my body. Goosebumps form all over my skin, little tingles following the path of his eyes. I'm confident with myself, and in my appearance. My mum and dad raised Hope and me to be comfortable in our own skin. I mean, if I look half as good as my mum does at her age, I would consider myself blessed. Because my mum is still bloody rockin' it.

"If I knew all I had to do was turn a shower on to get you naked so quickly, I would have done it sooner." Alex smirks, still perusing my body like he's a kid in a candy store and doesn't know which piece of me he wants most.

"Shut up and get undressed. I've had images of you in the shower playing on repeat in my head for two days. I am not missing my opportunity to put myself into that fantasy." I step around him and walk straight under the water.

Alex tilts his head. His hand on his chin, he says, "You know, I gave you one hell of a show through that window. It's only fair if you repay the favour."

"You want me to give you a show?" I ask, reaching for a bottle of bodywash. I squirt some into my palms and begin rubbing the soap along my breasts. "You want to stand there and watch as I rub myself down?"

Alex swallows as he licks his lips, his eyes not leaving my chest. I slowly trail one hand down, over my stomach, heading straight for my clit. I spread my legs further apart. "You want to watch while I bring myself pleasure, Alex? Watch... while I imagine that it's your hands on my body right now? That it's your fingers entering my tight little pussy right now," I breathe. Holy fuck, what started off as teasing *him* is now turning *me* the fuck on. I think I might like this little taste of voyeurism.

Alex, on the other hand, can't handle the heat. He slams my back against the wall. Before I know it, he's on his knees in front of me, his face buried between my legs. He brings one leg up to rest on his shoulder. His tongue dives in, circling around my clit. He moans into my mound.

My hands cling to the wet fabric of his shirt as I try to keep myself upright. "Oh God, Alex, don't stop." My screams drown out the sound of the running water. He answers by inserting two fingers into me while his mouth sucks on my clit, his tongue twirling in little circles.

Holy shit, he's good at this. How the hell does somebody get so damn good at this? I don't think I want to know—the thought kind of makes me want to take shooting lessons from Emily. She's scarily talented when it comes to target practice. No one has ever beaten her in a challenge yet. My dad has tried many times over the years—*he hates losing.*

Alex trails his other hand around my ass, and a finger starts pushing on that forbidden hole. My whole body stiffens. He's not actually going to...? Oh shit, he is. His finger pushes in. At the same time, he increases the speed of his tongue. I come apart; an orgasm hits me like a freight train.

"Holy shit!" What the fuck did he just do to me? I've never felt anything like that. I'm left a panting, whimpering mess when Alex stands. Unbuttoning his slacks, he frees himself from his pants.

"You good?" he asks.

"Better than good." Wrapping my arms around his neck, I swing my legs over his waist. He lines himself up and slams into me, with one solid, strong thrust. The force sends my back further into the wall. My head hits the tiles. I hear the crack, but I don't care.

"Shit, sorry. Are you okay?" He goes to step away, to put me on my feet.

"I swear if you stop right now, Alex, I will smother you in your sleep," I grit out. I use my pelvic floor muscles to clamp down around him. Every bit of me is clinging onto him, keeping him firmly embedded inside.

"Well, I'd hate to go out before I've had the chance to put a ring on you." He smiles as he begins to thrust. He's holding back though. *I can tell.* After a few minutes of his torturously slow movements, I crack.

"Alex, fuck me already, or I'll go find someone who

will." I have absolutely no intention of doing so. But my words elicit the exact reaction I was hoping for.

"Lily, I promise you, if you let another man touch you, I will fucking slaughter them. *After I torture them.* And I'll make you watch. Just so you think twice about doing such a thing again. This pussy. It's mine. This body of yours. It's now mine!" He growls as he thrusts, his efforts hard. *Forceful.* He's taking what's his.

"Who do you belong to, Lily?"

"Argh, myself," I moan.

"Wrong answer." He stops all movements. "Who the fuck do you belong to, Lily?"

"You, Alex, I'm yours!" As soon as the words leave my mouth, he starts up again. Harder and faster than before.

This is how I wanted to be fucked. *Like he owns me.* I'll even let him think he does. In the bedroom at least. For the second time tonight, I experience one hell of an intense orgasm. Alex is close behind me, calling out my name as he empties himself inside me.

"Wake up. Wake up. Wake up!" My dad's booming

voice pierces through my sleep fog. *My blissfully peaceful sleep fog.*

"Argh, make it stop. Just five more minutes." I roll over, covering my head with the blanket.

"Ah, Lil, about now would be a good time for you to take control of this boyfriend of yours. You know, before he shoots me." My dad laughs.

I bolt upright. And sure enough, Alex is sitting up in bed, gun in hand, with the barrel pointed straight at my dad. "What the hell, Alex? Put the gun down."

"Are you sure, Lily, because just now, you were begging me to make it stop." Alex lowers his weapon, tucking it back under his pillow.

"Normal people don't sleep with guns under their pillows. Get up! It's Christmas, and I'm not waiting for you two to open the gifts." My dad turns and walks out of the room.

"Why do you sleep with a gun under your pillow, Alex?" I know he's obviously not just a businessman, entrepreneur, or whatever crap he tried to feed me. But I need to hear it from him. What worries me is that I won't really care. I don't think it matters to me what he does. Well, unless he's selling kids or some horrible shit like that. If that were the case, I'd shoot him myself. Probably...

"Merry Christmas, Lily. I have something for you. Luckily, I had your gift in my pocket last night." He opens the bedside table and retrieves a black velvet box. *A little black velvet box.* The kind from a jewellery store. You know, like the ones you might open and find a ring inside.

Please do not let this be a ring. Oh fuck. What if it is. What do I say? Can I really do this, after just knowing someone for two days? It's completely insane, like Josh and Emily level insane. Holy cow, why am I even considering this? No, I can't do this. It's too soon.

"Lily, relax. Just open it," Alex says, as he covers my hands with his and opens the box.

A pair of the most stunning diamond and amethyst earrings shine back at me. I'm at a loss for words. "Alex, I-I don't know what to say. These are beautiful."

"You're welcome." He smirks.

"Thank you." I immediately remove what now seem like boring diamond studs, replacing them with the new pair. "I'm never taking these off," I tell him.

"I'm glad you like them. They look good. I think they'd look better if you lost the clothes."

"Mmm, I'm sure they would. But if we don't get out there, my dad will be back in here in five minutes. He gets a little crazy on Christmas."

"A little? Lily, my house looks like a scene from *The Nightmare Before Christmas*." He gets up and walks into an attached room. I follow him, and my breath catches in my throat.

It's not just any old room. It's the freaking motherload of all closets. "Oh my God! Alex, this is your closet?" I ask the obvious.

"Ah, yeah? Why? Do you think you'll need more

space? I can build you a bigger one." He pulls a black shirt down and puts it over his head. He's now wearing a loose pair of grey shorts and a fitted black t-shirt. How does he look this good so effortlessly? It's not fair.

"Ah, why would I need space?" I'm confused by his question.

"For when you move your things in?" He swaggers over to where I'm standing in the doorway. *Yes, he freaking swaggers.*

"Ah, I'm not moving in here, Alex." I have my own little apartment near the university campus. I love it. It's within walking distance of the Sydney aquarium, a place I visit often.

"Yes, you are." Alex folds his arms over his chest, his voice firm.

"No, I'm not!" I say just as firmly. Turning on my heel, I go to storm out, but his arms wrap around my stomach. I know I shouldn't, but I can't help it. It's almost like a natural response. I stomp on his foot and throw my elbow back into his ribs.

He groans and bends. But his grip on me doesn't falter. "Fuck, Lily. Really?" He grunts as he effortlessly picks me up off the floor. The next thing I know, I'm on the bed on my back, with Alex straddling my legs. "Do not try any of your ninja shit on me, Lily. I will not be happy if you hurt yourself on Christmas."

"What makes you think I'd be the one hurt?" I smile at him and let my body relax. I thought he'd lose his guard and loosen the grip he has on my wrists, which he's currently holding above my head. But he doesn't.

"I don't fight clean, Lily. I'll do anything to win. Anything to get what I want. And right now, what I want is for you to agree to move in with me." He starts trailing kisses up my neck, nibbling on the spot just behind my ear.

"Mmm." I slam my mouth shut; my body is betraying me. *I don't like this. I'm not enjoying this.* If I repeat the mantra enough, it will be true. Hopefully. "I'd love to move in with you, Alex," I say. He lifts his head and smiles down at me. "But your house is just too far away from uni, and it's nowhere near the aquarium, so I don't think it's going to be a viable option for me right now."

The frown returns to his face. "Uni? You'll have a driver every day, Lil. You won't have to worry about the commute," he offers.

"And what about the aquarium? I spend a lot of time there. I can't imagine living this far away."

"I'll build you a fucking aquarium in the house," he grumbles.

I laugh. There is no way he's building me a damn aquarium. "Okay, but we really do need to get out there." I point to the door, where I can hear a mixture of Christmas carols, laughter, and arguing. All the sounds of my family on Christmas morning.

"Let's do this. Just... on a scale from one to ten, how bad would it be if I end up shooting one of your family members today?" He picks up the handgun from under his pillow, tucking it behind his shorts.

"Ten! Alex, a huge freaking ten!" I yell. Is he crazy? "Do you think the Christmas tree is going to rob you or something? What do you need that for?"

"The first time I had dinner with your family, one of your aunts shot your cousin. The second time, my house blew up. I'm starting to think your family get-togethers are fucking cursed."

"Okay, but Emily's not my aunt—which is a fact I'm sure Ash and Bree are very thankful for, considering they're bumping uglies. And if it weren't for my family, you would have been in *that* house. You know, the one that blew up," I counter.

"You're right. Sorry, but you can never be too care-ful. Let's try to enjoy Christmas. It's our first of many to come, babe." Alex wraps an arm around my shoulder, leading me out of the room and through the house that does in fact look like a bad Christmas movie scene.

14

Alex

This house has never been so fucking loud. Lily's family is intense when it comes to Christmas. I wonder if I can convince her into having an overseas holiday next year, just the two of us. *Alone.* All I want to do is be alone with her, get her as addicted to me as I'm becoming to her.

"Took your time getting down here. Long night?" Lily's cousin, Dominic, greets her with a hug, while glaring at me. *Guess I'm not his favourite person this morning.*

"Well, you know, when your neighbour's house blows up, and you suddenly have to relocate on Christmas Eve, it kind of ends up being a long night, Dom." I don't like the answer Lily gives him. Really? Her *neighbour's* house?

"So, is he your neighbour, or your boyfriend, Lil Pill? Because, from the way he's looking right now, I don't think he's very happy," Dominic says, backing away from her.

Lily spins around and tilts her head up at me. "What's wrong?"

"Nothing," I grumble, walking into the kitchen. I need coffee, and so does she. I made sure there'd be a shitload of almond milk, along with a heap of vegan-friendly groceries for her.

"You know, usually it's the girl who says nothing's wrong, when obviously there *is* something wrong." Lily follows me into the kitchen and leans against the bench.

"Almond cap, right?" I try to change the topic; hopefully she'll forget all about it.

"Please." I can feel her eyes burning into my back. "Alex, just tell me. What's wrong? Is it too much? I know my family can be... a lot to handle. Trust me, I know that. And if you want us to leave, just say so."

"Lily, you leaving this house is the last thing I want. I just asked you to move in with me, less than five minutes ago. And I'm sure I can handle your family for one day."

"You're moving in together? Oh, I can't wait until Uncle Bray hears about this. Maybe it'll be what finally cracks him. He's been way too cool, calm, and collected about you two. It's bloody weird." A little pocket rocket of blonde hair twirls into the kitchen—*literally twirls.* I know this is one of Lily's cousins. I just can't for the life of me remember her name.

"Why are you twirling around in my kitchen?" I ask her.

"Because this house, these floors, are freaking amazing. They deserved to be danced on."

"Ava, seriously? It's too early for this. Can't you... I don't know... be normal and not so energetic in the morning?" Lily groans.

"I could, but why would I? So, you moving in or not? Dom said this guy's just the neighbour. Is it like a holiday fling? It'd be a shame not to be able to dance through this house again." Ava pouts.

"Well, as much as my dating life might interest you, it's none of your bloody business. Get out!" Lily frowns at her cousin.

"Oh, my dad sent me in here to tell you guys to hurry up. Gift time is about to start, as soon as Ash and Breanna make an appearance. Although, Dad went to wake Ash up about ten minutes ago—guess he found more than he bargained for." Ava twirls out of the room the same way she entered it.

"Here. And just an FYI: *this* is not coffee. Coffee is not meant to taste like shit." I hand her a mug of the worst coffee known to mankind. I tried it—won't be making that mistake again. It's like fucking cardboard.

"You're not, you know." Lily takes the cup, bringing it straight to her lips.

"I'm not what?"

"Just the neighbour." She smiles.

"Oh yeah? What else am I?"

"Well, you're the hot neighbour I caught masturbating in his shower." She laughs.

"Oh, you mean the one you stood there and watched, like a Peeping Tom. The whole time."

"Yep! There's no shame in my game, Alex."

"Okay, so I've been upgraded from just the neighbour to the hot neighbour. That's great."

"Well, I mean, you're also my new favourite barista."

I stare at her. She's fucking with me right now, and it's fucking working.

"Lily, how many hot barista neighbours give you a quarter of a mil worth of diamond earrings for Christmas?" I ask with my eyebrows raised.

"What? Holy shit, Alex, no! You did not. Are you nuts? That's insane. Holy shit, Alex."

"I think that's quickly becoming my new favourite phrase. *Holy shit, Alex* has a ring to it." I smirk. It's the same thing she screams in the bedroom.

"Stop. You should take them back. I can't accept

something so expensive. I thought they were freaking costume jewellery, Alex." She puts her coffee cup on the bench and reaches up for her ear.

Taking hold of her wrists, I raise them above her head. Her hands lean against the overhead cabinets. "Lily, ask me?"

"Ask you what?"

"Ask me who you are to me?"

"Who am I to you?"

"Well, at the moment, you're my annoyingly stubborn girlfriend, who in a very short time is going to be my annoyingly stubborn fiancée. Who will then become my annoyingly stubborn, beautiful wife. But most importantly, Lily, you are mine."

"Mmm, maybe we should take it one day at a time, and keep the girlfriend title around for a while. I've never had a boyfriend as hot as you are, and I want to flaunt you to all my friends. Kinda like a trophy boyfriend."

"I think I like trophy *husband* better. But, today, I'm happy with boyfriend." I'm not fucking happy with the boyfriend title, but it's a huge improvement from *the hot neighbour guy.*

"Okay, if you're not in here, I'm keeping your gifts," Bray shouts from the living room. I pick up Lily's coffee, grab her hand, and walk into the living room. The moment we enter, everyone stops what they are doing and stares at us.

"Ahh, oh my God, my baby's in love!" Reilly jumps

up and charges at Lily. I have to put my hand on her back to prevent her from toppling over.

"Oh, it's so freaking cute. Why don't you ever say sweet shit like that to me?" Alyssa looks to Zac before coming towards Lily. *What the fuck is going on?*

"I can't believe it, the first one to fall. I've been waiting for this moment my whole life." Ella is next to hug Lily.

I pull Lily against my side. "Did I miss something? Did you win the Nobel Prize or something?" I whisper to her.

"I have no freaking idea what's happening," she whispers back.

"Okay, so I'm thinking a spring wedding. It'll be beautiful. All the flowers. The dress. Oh my God, Lily, the dress!" Reilly's screech pierces my damn eardrums.

"Okay, stop! You heard her. They're taking it slow, which is the smart thing to do, Lil," Bray shouts above the squealing women.

"Lily, when you and Uncle Alex get married, can I be a flower girl?" Tessie asks, peering up at us.

I smile. "*Bella*, you're going to be the most beautiful flower girl the world has ever seen," I tell her.

"Yes, Mummy, did you hear? Uncle Alex said I can be a flower girl." Tessie runs over to Mia, who doesn't seem as thrilled with the idea.

"Okay. This one's for—oh! It says Tessie. Is there anyone named Tessie here?" Bray asks as he pulls a gift out from the tree, in a blatant attempt to move everyone on from talking about my upcoming nuptials.

Two hours, it's taken two hours to get through each gift under the tree. I don't know how they managed it, but Lily's family delivered on Christmas for Tessie. I had my men go to the shops last night to pick up some shit, so she'd have *something* to open. I wasn't sure how I was going to explain to a five-year-old that all her gifts blew up with the house.

But between the Williamsons and the McKinleys, Tessie is going to need a whole other bedroom just for the gifts she's received today. She is totally worn out now, lounging on the couch with the brand-new iPad Josh got her. It's odd that I haven't even thought about the merger deal with him over the past twenty-four hours. Well, not much anyway. Business is always in the back of my mind.

"Lily, I'm going to get a drink. You want anything?"

"Coffee?" she asks.

"Sure, be right back. Don't disappear on me." I kiss her forehead and head to the kitchen.

"You know, if you hurt her, I will kill you. I don't care who you are, or how important you think you may be." Fuck, Josh... Of all people's threats, his is one I don't take lightly. I know he means every fucking word. Am I running scared? Fuck no. He can come at me with all he's got; he hasn't seen me yet. He may think he has, may think he knows me, but he'd be dead fucking wrong.

"If I ever hurt her, I'll cut my own heart out," I tell him honestly.

"You know, at first, I thought you were using her, getting close to her to get closer to me."

"What makes you so sure I'm not?" I counter. I'm not. *I wouldn't.* But I need to know what it is he thinks he knows.

"I know blind love when I see it. You and her, it's the real deal." He shrugs. "I've instructed my assistant to set up a meeting a week from today. The merger will go through. Congratulations, you're now in business with McKinley Industries."

"Huh, I should be the one congratulating you. You're now in business with The Mancini Corporation." I shake his offered hand.

"I've done a lot of digging, Alessandro. I know enough to bring your organisation to its knees. Don't think, for even a second, that I won't." Josh walks to the doorway, then stops. "One more thing. If you don't tell her who you really are, what you really do, *I will.* And trust me, that won't bode well for you."

15

Lily

I can't believe I'm doing this. I'm actually considering moving in with Alex. A guy I met just two days ago. It's completely insane. It's worse than insane. It's straight-jacket wearing, padded-cell level crazy. But the thought of going home after today, without him, is not sitting well with me.

Everyone's busy fidgeting and messing around with their gifts. Tessie is exhausted and sprawled out on a sofa with an iPad. Mia is sitting next to her, sporadically sending me weird-ass glares. I don't know what I've done to her. I'll figure that out later.

"Are you really considering this, Lil. It's too soon," Hope whispers.

"I know that, but I can't explain it. I don't know what's wrong with me... I literally think about going home without him, and my chest tightens up on me."

"I know. I feel it too. Do me a favour and stop thinking about it. Your confused, depressed feelings are running straight from you to me." She always complains that she hates how we feel each other so much. It's a weird twin thing. But I know she wouldn't change it for the world. And neither would I.

"I mean, he *is* hot. Imagine your babies, Lil. Fucking gorgeous little critters, they'd be."

"Did you just refer to my future children as *critters*? Aunt of the year material." I laugh.

"I know I'll be the favourite. How could I not be?" She shrugs. "Do you think we'll ever have what they have?" Hope asks, pointing to our parents, aunts, and uncles.

"I think I might have found it, Hope, and it's scaring the shit out of me. What if I can't do it? What if all these things I'm feeling are one-sided? Maybe it's all in my head. I should probably go. Just leave now while everyone's distracted, and avoid a scene of pure embarrassment when Alex changes his mind about me."

My dad glares at me from across the room with that

weird "I know what you're thinking" look he has. *Nope, not dealing with this now.* I need to get out of here. "Hope, do whatever you can to distract everyone. I'm out," I whisper, getting up as calmly as I can.

I hear Hope scream "spider," followed by her high-pitched shouts for someone to get it. It works—everyone knows her fear of spiders is not to be taken lightly. With the number of times we've played on that fear as a distraction technique, I wonder how no one's noticed it yet. I pull the front door open, only to be greeted by a towering silhouette wider than the threshold.

"Going somewhere?" the overly muscular, steroid-induced hulk of a man asks.

"Yes, so I'd appreciate it if you moved."

"Sorry, no can do, until I clear it with the boss." He has his phone to his ear before I can even comprehend what he just said. *Clear it with the boss?* What the hell is there to clear? Does he think we're prisoners here? If Alex thinks he can keep me locked up in this house, he's going to have to tie me down—*literally tie me to his bed*. Shit, that's not entirely unappealing, now that I think about it. What the hell is wrong with me?

"Yeah, boss, got a redhead at the front door, wanting to leave." I don't hear the response he receives from whom I have to assume is Alex.

"What's your name?" the hulk asks me.

"Ah, Hope." I try to say it quietly, so Alex doesn't hear my voice.

The hulk listens, then pockets his phone again. "Boss said to wait here."

"Excuse me?" What the hell? Like fuck I'm waiting here. "Never mind, I'll find another way out of this stupid house." When I turn around, an angry-looking Alex is marching across the foyer and straight towards me. He doesn't say anything as he reaches me, just clasps his hand in mine and takes me outside. "Alex, what are you doing?"

"We're walking *out of my stupid house*—it seems."

Shit, he heard that. "Sorry, I didn't mean that your house is stupid."

"No? Did you mean to leave without saying so much as a goodbye? Fuck, Lily, you were going to leave your whole family in my house on Christmas Day and just disappear? How do you think that would have gone down? It's almost lunchtime. Did you think you wouldn't have been missed by, hell, everyone?" He's fuming. His grip on my hand tightens to the point it fucking hurts.

I pull on my arm. He loosens his grip but doesn't let go. Instead, he keeps walking. I didn't get a chance to see just how beautiful this property was last night. The gardens are spectacular.

"Hope would have made an excuse for me." Even as I say it, I know how lame it sounds.

"Okay, well, for future reference, Hope's excuses won't cut it for me. If you're missing, and I don't know where you are, don't think there would be a stone left unturned until I found you."

I don't know what to say to that. When it's just Alex and me, in the rare moments we've been alone, I get so lost in him I almost forget myself. I get so carried away in these feelings he evokes within me I can't think of ever not being with him. But that's stupid crazy.

Alex stops at the wooden swing overlooking a large pond. The sun is shining down and reflecting off the water. I can feel the heat of the day already colouring my skin. I really can't stay out here for long. I'll end up looking like a tomato.

I sit down on the swing. Alex still has a strong grasp on my hand. "What are you trying to run away from, Lily? Did something happen? Did someone say something to you?"

"I'm not running. I just... I don't know... I felt like I should leave."

"Why?"

"I don't know. *This...*" I point between the two of us. "It's too intense, Alex. I just met you, and you're talking about me moving in—*about getting married.* It's been two days. It's crazy intense. I just... I don't know. What happens if, say I go along with your craziness and move in. Then next week, when the holidays are over, you wake up realising you made a mistake. What if this is just meant to be a holiday fling?"

His face screws up like he's disgusted over what I just said. "This isn't a fling, Lily. I don't do flings. I know what I want. And I always go after it with everything I have. I'm sorry if I've scared you off by being too intense. I don't know how to do *this*. I haven't ever had to do *this* before."

"What? Date someone?"

"We're beyond dating, Lily."

"Are we? We haven't actually had a first date."

"You want to go on a date with me, Lily? Because if it's wining and dining you need, I assure you *I will deliver*."

"It's not that I need to be wined and dined. But we need to slow down. Get to know each other. I have some really bad habits, you know. Ones that, when you discover them, will have you thinking twice about living with me."

"Oh yeah, like what? You pick your nose? You leave the toilet seat up?"

"Ew, no. But I'm messy. Like really messy. I leave clothes everywhere, shoes, handbags... I always lose my car keys. I'm never on time. And I like to bake, but I hate doing dishes."

"That's all? I have maids, Lily. I don't care how messy you are. I have staff to drive you anywhere you need to go."

"Do you always have an answer for everything?" I ask him.

"I try to."

"There's also my family; they're overly involved in my life. Like always around. *Always.* I moved out to get away. Yet, somehow, they all ended up with keys to my apartment."

"You know, this has been the best Christmas Mia and I have had in forever. You are lucky to have the family you do. Not everyone has that."

"What happened to your parents?"

"Nothing happened to them. As far as I'm aware, they are still rotting away in the trailer park Mia and I left behind. I didn't have the same kind of childhood as you, Lily. I've done a lot of stuff I don't exactly regret, to get to where I am today. I still do a lot of stuff I won't apologise for."

"Like what? What is it that you do, exactly, Alex?"

"I have many legitimate businesses." His hand tightens around mine, like he's afraid I'm going to run for the hills. "I also have some not-so-legitimate ones."

"Am I going to wake up one day to you being arrested?"

"Not likely. Lily, I'm currently at the top of the underground world here. I have politicians and police in my corner. Everyone wants something. But with all those assets I have on my side, I have just as many people trying to bring me down."

I look out over the pond. How do I react to being told my boyfriend is a criminal? Not just any old criminal, but the head criminal? If that's what you'd call it. I should care, right? I should tell him to let me go. The problem is... I don't know if I want him to.

It's really peaceful here, but so damn hot I'm tempted to jump in the water. It looks clean enough.

"I have one question—well, I have a few. But there's only one I want to ask you now."

"You can ask me anything. I may not always be able to answer, but I'll do my best."

"Would you follow me anywhere?" Right now, I feel like I'd follow him blindly. I want to know if the sentiment is mutual or not.

"I would," he says, after pondering the question for a few minutes.

"Good." I twist my arm around until he has to let go of my hand. I jump up and strip my dress over my head while Alex stares, wide-eyed. Dropping the material to the grass, I run into the pond, the water instantly cooling my skin.

"Lily, what the bloody hell are you doing? Get the fuck out of there."

I pout at him. "But I thought you said you'd follow me anywhere. If you want me to get out, you're going to have to come and get me yourself." I float around the water. There's little fish skimming the surface, but that doesn't bother me.

"Are you nuts? There're creatures living in there, Lily. I can see things swimming around your legs. Get out! That water's going to make you sick; it can't be clean," he growls.

"Well, I guess you really should come and get me then. Because I'm a really, really crappy sick person.

You do not want to experience that this early on in our relationship."

"Fuck!" He curses as he bends to undo his shoes. He strips his shirt off and tentatively walks into the water. I purposely float further away from him.

"Lily, stop. Don't move. I'm coming in, against my better judgement. And if I get sick from this filthy water, you'll be nursing me back to health. In a sexy little nurse's outfit and all." He continues to curse under his breath, until he finally reaches me.

"Oh shit. Alex, don't move!" I raise my voice. His whole body freezes. He frantically looks around in the water.

"What is it? What the fuck is in here?" he shouts.

I burst out laughing as I wrap myself around his body. "Nothing. Gosh, you are such a sook. Who would have thought the big, bad Alessandro Mancini would be such a scaredy pants?"

"Not funny, Lily. We're getting out of here now." He wraps his arms around my back, holding me in place, as he exits the pond at a much quicker pace than he entered it.

16

Alex

By the time we make it back to the house, everyone is on the patio and seated around the table. I was hoping I could sneak through this way before anyone saw us, then go and shower the pond muck off our bodies. I shiver at the thought of what could be living in that fucking filthy water. I can't believe Lily would be so careless as to just jump in.

What if I had a pet water snake or some other weird shit in there?

We are drenched. Lily put her dress back on, but the wetness from her bra and panties has soaked through, causing the material to cling to her body. Her hair's dripping down her back. Yet, when I look at her, she doesn't seem to have a care in the world. Her smile is fucking huge as she approaches the table. There are only two seats left, and they're not fucking next to each other. One of them is at the head of the table, with Mia and Leo sitting on each side. The seat that's always reserved for me. I can't *not* sit there. It would send the wrong fucking message to my men.

I'm the head of this organisation. I have to be seated at the head of the table. But there's no way in hell I'm *not* sitting next to Lily. What I'm about to do is going to make a statement—a huge fucking statement —to everyone, especially my men. They will all get the message that Lily is worth more to me than anyone else.

My steps falter as I walk around the table to the only vacant chair. If I do this, it will put a huge fucking target on her back. I have many enemies. And if I don't, I'm implying she's not important enough to be seated next to me. I'm damned if I do, damned if I don't. The thought of not sitting next to her though, that thought alone has me picking up the chair, carrying it around the table, and placing it down right next to mine.

I nod my head for Lily to sit. She stares back at me,

wide-eyed. Everyone else around the table has gone quiet, looking to see what happens next. This is unheard of. I'm surprised Lily would know the hidden meaning behind my actions. But the look on her face tells me she has no doubt.

"Lily, don't overthink it. Sit down," I growl into her ear. She shivers before smiling at me and taking her seat. I tuck her chair in. Nodding my head to one of the servers, I tell him to arrange another place setting before I take my own seat. Everyone is still quiet, staring at Lily and me. "Did someone die?" I ask.

"Not yet, but the night's young," Ash answers with a cocky smirk.

"Okay, let's eat then. I'm starving," I say, and right on cue, the servers come out with the entrees.

There's a range of share platters, containing seafood, cold meats, and cheeses as well as a variety of other finger foods. I told the catering company to ensure there were plenty of vegan options. When I pick up Lily's plate and fill it with a mixture of fruits, vegies, vegan cheeses, and crackers, I notice everyone is still looking at us.

I place the dish in front of her. "Is there anything else you want, babe?" I ask, giving her my full attention. I don't give a fuck about having an audience. The blush rises from Lily's neck all the way up to her cheeks. She's not fond of having everyone's eyes on her.

"Well, fuck me! I think Christmas is going to be at

Alex's every year. This spread is epic! Alex, you're now my favourite of all of Lily's boyfriends," Hope yells out from her spot in the middle of the table as she starts piling up her plate. Although I know she's said that to get the attention off Lily, the fact that she mentioned Lily's other boyfriends has me grinding my molars together.

"Hope, watch your language. And Lily hasn't ever had any fucking boyfriends before. Have you, princess?" Bray looks pointedly at Lily.

She shrugs her shoulders as she mumbles, "None you've met." *That* has my head turning to face her.

"I'm gonna need a list of names."

"You'll die waiting for that list, Alex. Besides, I'm sure mine's way shorter than yours."

Mia bursts out laughing. The glare I send her does nothing to hold her back. Once she composes herself, she looks to Lily. "So, Lily, what are your intentions with my brother?"

"Mia, shut it," I growl.

"Nope. If I suddenly brought a guy home, along with a shitload of extended family, you'd be asking a lot more questions." Mia smirks. "No offense," she adds, looking down the table at our aforementioned guests.

The room fills with chatter, everyone breaking off into their own conversations. Lily looks at me before answering Mia's question.

"Well, right now, my intentions are to eat until I'm

in a food coma. Then, tonight, my intentions are purely R-rated—I'm not sure you really want to know about them. But my intentions for tomorrow? To do it all again, I suppose." Lily shrugs.

"Can we press fast-forward to tonight?" I suggest.

"Ew, gross. As long as you know… if you break his heart, I'll rip yours right out of your chest." Mia smiles.

"Mia! A word." Rising to my feet, I storm towards the doors leading back inside the house. "Now!" I yell when I notice she is not following me. I wait until she walks through the door before slamming it. Grabbing hold of Mia's elbow, I drag her into the kitchen. "Out!" The catering staff each drops what they're doing to make a hasty escape.

"What the hell, Alex? Let me go." Mia wiggles out of my grasp.

"What's your problem, Mia? Who do you think you are, threatening Lily like that?"

"Who do I think *I* am? Your fucking sister, idiot. It's my job to protect you, Alex. You've got your panties all up in a twist over this girl. You only met her two days ago, and you've practically moved her in." Mia throws her hands up in frustration.

"You may be my sister, but that does not give you the right to talk to Lily like that. You will show her the same respect you show me."

"No, I won't. Not until I feel she deserves it. You can sit her next to you all you want, but she needs to prove she's worthy of that seat."

"No! She doesn't need to prove shit to anyone. My word is all you need. Mia, I swear to God, if I ever hear you threaten her again, you won't like the consequences," I growl, running my hands through my hair.

"You're going to choose a piece of ass over me? Alex, it's always been us, you and me. We look out for each other. We don't bloody well need anyone else."

"I'd never choose anyone over you, Mia. You're my sister. You will always be my person. But, so help me God, if you try to come between Lily and me..." I let my sentence trail off. What would I actually do? She's my sister. I'd never hurt a hair on her head. "Just don't put me in this position again. I know it's fast, but I've never felt this way before. I know she's my one."

"I'm sorry. I'll try to bite my tongue next time I want to go all *protective little sister* on you." She smiles.

I wrap my arms around her. "Thank you."

"But you have to promise that, when I decide I'm ready to date again, you will stay out of my dating life too."

"Yeah, that's probably never going to happen."

"We should get back out there," Mia whispers. "Hopefully your little temper tantrum didn't scare her off."

"Fuck! Let's go. Wait, you don't think...? No, Lily is tougher than you realize, Mia. She doesn't scare so easily. She swims with sharks, for fuck's sake. *Willingly.*" When we make it back to the table, no one bothers to look up as we take our seats. Wrapping my arm behind the back of Lily's chair, I lean into her. "You okay?"

"Yep, you?" Her eyes search mine.

"I am now. Sorry about my sister. She's a little over-protective... at times." I smirk.

"I know all about overprotective sisters—*don't worry*."

The rest of Christmas lunch went off without a hitch. No one got shot, so I'm counting that as a win. After lunch, Lily's extended family filled their cars and left. My house still looks like Christmas threw up all over every fucking surface. But I have Lily here, along with her sister and parents, so I'm trying my best to ignore the chaos.

It's late afternoon, and I'm sitting by the pool. Lily said she'd meet me out here about fifteen minutes ago. I'm watching the door like a hawk, waiting for the moment she exits so I can jump on her. Only she doesn't arrive alone, like I was hoping.

"Sorry. Took me a while to locate where you hide the good stuff. Then I found Mia and, well, we had to sample the goods before we decided on what to bring. I can totally afford to replace this though, so don't stress. Wait... you don't mind, do you? Shit, I should have asked first, shouldn't I?" Lily rambles on as she stumbles forward, holding up a bottle of my five-thou-sand-dollar whiskey. Hope and Mia tumble out behind her, in a similar if not worse state.

"Are you drunk? All of you?" I ask them, standing

and taking the bottle from Lily's hands before she fucking drops it.

"Not drunk, but close. Maybe drunk-*ish*. Is that the word, Lil?" Hope asks, looking towards her twin.

"I don't know. Why are you asking me?"

"Because you're the smart twin. I'm the pretty one." Hope shrugs.

"That doesn't work when you look exactly the same," Mia interjects, swiping the bottle from my hands and sitting down on one of the loungers. Lily and Hope quickly follow suit.

"Where's Tessie, Mia?" I ask.

"Oh, she was asleep on the couch in the theatre. Bray and Reilly are watching her."

Lily's parents are babysitting my niece? That's fucking weird. I should go in there. But I can't exactly leave these three drunks by the pool—*by themselves*—either. "Okay, you need water. Let me call for some." I take the bottle from Mia, holding it out of her reach.

"You know, you used to be cool, Alex, then you got old," she grumbles.

"Wait, how old are you?" Lily asks.

"I'm not fucking old," I growl. I didn't want the age-gap thing to come up yet.

"How old is not old?" she pushes.

"Twenty-nine," my sister answers for me.

"Huh, that's not old, Mia. Besides, he's got the stamina of a young stallion."

"Ew, gross. Never say that to me again, Lily." Mia scrunches her face up.

"Well, Alex." Lily stands and wraps her arms around my neck, rubbing her bikini clad-body over mine. "You can either join us, or leave us," she whispers as she nibbles on my ear.

I didn't notice until after she had done it. The little minx just got that bottle out of my hands, using her art of seductive distraction. What the fuck? I am not that easily fooled.

"I'm not getting drunk with you, Lily. Who would be the responsible sober one if I did?"

Lily lies down on an empty lounger. She takes the cap off the bottle and then proceeds to pour the amber liquid over her breasts. "Oops, I think I spilled some. Maybe I should see if anyone's available to help me clean myself up?" She winks at me.

That's an invitation I'm not stupid enough to turn down. Not caring that both of our sisters are in the room, I lower my body over hers as I run my tongue along the exposed skin of her breasts.

"And that's my cue. Hope, let's go. I'll show you where the good spots are for perving on my brother's men." Mia grabs Hope's hand and leads her out of the room.

As soon as the doors shut, I pull on the little strings holding up Lily's bikini top. Rolling the material to uncover her nipples, I watch as she pours more of my fucking whiskey over one, then the other. And I can't think of a better accompaniment for my favourite liquor.

My mouth closes around her nipple. Her body arches up into me as she drops the bottle on the ground. Her hands tug on my hair, holding my head to her breast. "Mmm, you taste so fucking good," I mumble around a mouthful.

"Pretty sure that's the whiskey."

"No, that's all you, babe. You are the most intoxicating thing I've ever consumed."

"Mmm, less talking, more licking, sucking, biting." My hand trails down to tug at the ties along each of her hips. They come apart way too fucking easily. I need to remember to burn this fucking bikini when I'm finished with her. My tongue licks down her stomach, swirling around her belly button before her hands pull me back up. "I need you inside me now, Alex," she demands.

"I think you've forgotten who's in control here, Lily. You don't get to call the shots." Although my mind means every word I say, my cock is arguing with me, demanding I give into her commands.

"Argh, Alex, if you don't put that bloody dick of yours inside me, I'm going to..." Her words die when I pinch her clit. "Oh God!" she screams out as her pelvis tilts upwards.

"Now, you're going to stop being a mouthy little brat, and let me lick this greedy fucking pussy of yours like the good girl you are," I tell her as I start my descent down south again.

I don't make it far. Somehow, a tipsy Lily still has fucking moves. She ends up on top of me, her hands freeing my cock from my boardshorts before the shock has even worn off. She leans over me, lining up her entrance. She's never looked sexier. I fucking love when she takes control.

"There's something you should probably know about me, Alex," she says, still hovering above my tip but not yet sinking down.

"What's that, babe?" I raise an eyebrow.

"I always get what I want." She slowly lowers herself onto me.

"Guess what?" I ask her, thrusting up while gripping my hands on her waist.

"What?" she moans as she circles her hips.

"So do I." I pick her up, bringing her legs to rest on each side of my face. She lets out a gasp as I lower her pussy to my mouth, running my tongue along her slit. Her body falls forward as she grips the back of the lounger.

"Fuck me! Why the hell didn't I just let you do this first? God, you're good at this," Lily says as she shamelessly rides my face.

I growl into her mound, licking, biting, and sucking down every last drop of her juices. My palms dig into the flesh of her ass. One finger finds her asshole before slowly entering. She screams my name as her body seizes and she comes.

I don't give her time as I roll out from under her. Standing behind her, I position her on her knees before slamming my cock forward. One of my hands wraps around her hair, tugging her head towards me. Leaning over, I close my mouth over hers.

"Mmm, oh God! I can't," Lily cries into my mouth.

"You can, and you will," I grunt, as I straighten up and thrust into her like the crazed animal she makes me. "Your cunt was fucking made for me, Lily. So perfect, tight, wet, warm, and fucking greedy for my cock." Her walls tighten and her juices flood my cock as my words echo through the room. Reaching a hand beneath her, I rub circles around her clit. My balls tighten. I can feel the orgasm building up, the tingles running up my spine. "You need to come for me now, Lily. Now, damn it!" I growl. "I want it. Give it to me!"

Her body obeys me perfectly, and her pussy milks my cock for everything it's got.

17

Lily

It's New Year's Eve. How has it only been a week since I met Alex? We haven't spent a day apart from each other yet. He even came with me to my apartment today when I said I had to actually go home. He doesn't like that I'm not officially moved in with him. He asks me every day, but I'm not giving up my apartment just yet.

As much as I want to take that leap, make the jump

into the unknown, I can't. I need to be smart about this relationship. It's new. It can't be healthy to move in with each other after just one week, can it?

We've had the best couple of days in the Hunter Valley. After spending Boxing Day at the McKinley Ranch with the rest of my family, Alex whisked me off to a resort. We spent two days wine tasting, eating cheese, and having sex on every available surface we could find. It was bliss.

We returned to the city yesterday. I spent most of the day catching up on sleep while Alex worked. I'm not entirely sure how I feel about his type of work just yet. Alex has questioned why I'm not running for the hills, and why I'm not shocked or disgusted by what he does. I haven't told him it's probably because—whatever it is he does—I'm certain my cousins on my mum's side have done one hundred times worse.

Hope and I don't exactly advertise that we're cousins of the mafia. It's bad enough growing up with Ash always in our business. I'm thankful that my other cousins live in New York. If they were here, there is no way they would approve of Alex. And as much manpower as Alex has surrounding him, it won't ever be enough to hold off those crazy bastards.

I'm digging through my wardrobe, trying to find an outfit for tonight. Pulling out a hot little sparkly black dress, I hold it up against myself in front of the mirror.

"No," Alex says. For a minute, I think he's talking to himself. He's sitting on my bed, typing away on his phone. I don't think he's even looked up at me. But when I go to put the dress in my overnight bag, he drops his phone and pulls the dress back out, repeating the singular word. "No."

"You can say *no* as much as you like, but that doesn't change the fact that I'm wearing *this* tonight." I snatch the dress from him and return it to the bag.

"Where are you planning on going tonight?" he asks, his eyebrows drawn down.

"It's New Year's Eve, Alex." I answer like that's all the explanation I need to give.

"I'm aware, so again, where is it you're planning on going?"

"The Merge. Hope and I always go there for New Year's Eve." I shrug.

"And when were you going to tell me about these plans?"

He's starting to piss me off with his line of questioning. Who does he think he is? I'm not ever going to ask his permission to go anywhere.

"You're not my father, Alex. If you think I'm going to ask for your permission, then you should go find yourself a mindless bimbo. Because that sure as shit isn't me."

The asshole smirks as his eyes rake up and down my body. "Thank fuck for that. I happen to love your mind, babe. No, you don't need to ask me for permission. What you need to do is give me a bit of notice, so I have time to arrange an appropriate security detail."

"It's my cousin's club. I don't need security. Besides, don't act like you're not coming with me."

"Thought you'd never ask. I'd love to accompany you tonight, sweetheart," he answers sarcastically. "And you're the girlfriend of Alessandro Mancini. You need a security detail."

I roll my eyes. Sometimes I think his ego is bigger than his cock. "You know, I'm more than capable of taking care of myself. I've been doing it for years."

"I'm sure you have. But now you don't need to, because I want to take care of you. Not because you can't, but because *I can*." He stands and wraps me in his arms, his woodsy scent engulfing me.

Damn it, he's smooth. I'll give him that. "Okay, I'll try to give you a heads-up next time. But I'm not ever going to ask permission for anything, Alex."

"I'd never want you to, Lily. You are my partner, my equal, my queen. Don't ever let anyone tell you otherwise."

The club is packed. People are crowded in, even up here in the VIP section. It's the busiest I've ever seen it.

Alex has not left my side all night. It's like his hand is glued to mine. I can tell he's not overly comfortable here. He keeps looking around, like he's waiting for something to jump out and attack.

"Let's do shots." Hope jolts up, clicking her fingers in the air at the server walking by.

"Tequila, *stat*," she yells at him when he approaches.

"Please," I add with a smile. The server smiles back as his eyes travel up the length of my legs. Alex stands, slowly, casually. I glance up at him in question, but he's not looking at me. He's looking at the man in front of us, who is still looking at my legs. I can't hear what he says, but when Alex leans in and whispers something to the server, the guy's face goes ash white. He nods his head with wide eyes before turning and literally running out of the VIP section.

Alex sits back down, just as casually as he stood up. "What did you say to him?" I ask.

"I told him that it'd take me ten seconds to gouge his eyes out of his head with my thumbs, before I made him swallow each one." Alex lifts my hand and brings it to his mouth, kissing my palm.

My jaw drops. I look to Hope to see if she over-heard our exchange. She didn't. She's too busy staring at the bar, where Chase is getting his flirt on with some blonde chick.

"Ah, Alex, that's... graphic." How am I meant to respond to something like that?

"It's honest. He shouldn't have been looking at you."

"I'll be back in a sec," Hope growls as she jumps to her feet.

"Oh shit. Hold my drink." I shove my glass at Alex as I follow Hope. I know that tone, and it only means one thing. She's about to get us both into trouble.

Hope walks right up to the blonde who has her hands all over Chase. I don't hear what Hope says to her, but I do see the blonde push at my sister's shoulder. *Yeah, that's not happening.* Even knowing my sister is the one in the wrong here—she has no claim over Chase—she's still my sister, and nobody touches my sister.

I walk up and swing, landing my knuckles square on the girl's jaw. The blonde stumbles back a bit. But before I can even think about swinging again, I'm surrounded by five men, all aiming guns in every direction, other than mine. Arms wrap around my waist from behind me, and without thinking, I jam my elbow back into a wall of muscle.

"Ah, shit, Lily. Why the fuck can't you hit like a girl?" Alex groans. Turning around, I smile at him.

"Because I'm Lily Hope Williamson—*that's why.*"

The crowd starts yelling, counting down from ten. Before they get to one, Alex drops his mouth to mine. He kisses me like we're the only ones here, like no one is watching. I love the way he kisses me, possesses me with every single touch, with every swirl of his tongue along mine. He tastes like whiskey, although I know he's been sipping the same drink all night.

"Happy New Year's," he says into my mouth.

"This is going to be the best year yet," I tell him.

"Oh yeah, why's that?"

"The year started with the perfect kiss. How can it not be the best?" The smile Alex gives me is huge, the kind of smile that reaches his eyes. Eyes that are usually hard as stone and set in a glare. By the time I turn around, the blonde is gone and Hope is playing tonsil hockey with Chase. I pull her off him before handing her to Alex, because she's way too drunk to be making smart choices right now. "Chase, where's Ash?" I ask.

Chase's smile widens. "He's not coming in tonight. He called earlier."

"What's wrong with him? He wouldn't just miss New Year's Eve," I ask, confused. My cousin is a bloody workhorse. He never takes a day off.

"No idea, but your boyfriend over there needs to let go of Hope. *Now*, Lily. I don't care who the fuck he is. If he doesn't let her go, I will make him," Chase growls.

I laugh. I know Chase can hold his own. But really? He'd go up against Alex for Hope?

"She's drunk, Chase. She doesn't know what she's doing. I'm taking her home."

"I'll take her home. I haven't been drinking, Lily," Chase offers. I look at him suspiciously. "Come on, Lil.

How long have we known each other? I'm not going to take advantage of her."

"It looked to me like you already were." I shrug.

"No, I wasn't." Chase stands, says something to the barkeeper on the other side of the counter, and walks straight up to Alex. Taking Hope's hand, he whispers into her ear. She nods her head and leans her body into his. This is going to end badly. *Very badly.* Alex gestures for one of his men, the one who always seems to be there. I watch the hushed exchange before the guy nods and looks at Hope.

"Chase is giving me a ride home, Lil. I'll call you tomorrow—or should I say *today*?" Hope says, wrapping her arms around me.

"Are you sure you want to get a ride from him?"

"More than you know." She laughs before tugging Chase down the stairs. I watch Alex's man follow them out.

Beep, beep, beep. "Shut it off, please!" I cover my head with the blanket.

"It's your phone, babe. It's been going off for a while." Alex's voice is rough from sleep.

"Tell them to go away," I complain, turning over and burying my face in his chest. If I have to be awake, at least I get to snuggle up to this body of his. What better way to start the day?

"It's Hope. She wants to talk to you." When I look up, he's holding the phone out to me, showing me my sister is on the other line.

"Hope, unless you're dying, I don't want to know," I grumble.

"Ash has a baby," she screams through the receiver.

"What?" I thought Breanna wasn't pregnant…

"Ash has a baby. A real-life baby girl. Mum says she got dropped off to the doorman with a note saying she belonged to Ash."

I bolt upright. "Ash has a baby?" I repeat, still not believing the words even as they leave my mouth.

"Yep, Chase told me. I called bullshit and dialled Mum. She said it's true. Uncle Zac and Aunt Lyssa spent the night at Ash's apartment."

"That's insane. Is it even his?"

"I don't know. I gotta go, but I'll call you in a bit." The phone cuts out before I can ask more questions. Jumping out of bed, I head into the wardrobe and throw on one of Alex's shirts, before I call my mum.

"Hey, Lil, guess your sister already called you?" she asks.

"Yep, is it true? Ash has a baby?"

"Yes, Lyssa sent me pictures. She's as cute as a button. Definitely a Williamson baby."

"Wow... what do I do? How do I help him?" This is way out of my element.

"I don't know. Maybe call Uncle Zac or Aunt Lyssa, see if they need anything. Your father and I just had a heap of stuff for the baby delivered this morning. Can you believe it? Someone actually leaving their baby with a father who knew nothing about the child? It's sad."

"Well, before Bree, Ash's standards obviously weren't very high."

18

Alex

We've just finished having three baby seats installed into three of Ash's cars, down in his garage. The guy really needs to up his security. It would have been way too easy for me, or one of the men I brought along with me, to drive straight out with any of these luxury vehicles.

Lily takes my hand and stabs a code into the buttons on the elevator. I don't question her. She's fuming. The red hue on her cheeks is not from being turned on. No, her jaw is clenched, her eyes squinted and focused on those doors like she's on a mission. She looks fucking hot as hell when she's mad. Now's probably not the best time to tell her that though, so I do the smart thing and keep my mouth shut.

As soon as the doors open, Lily squeezes my hand almost to the breaking point and stomps—literally stomps—through the foyer while yelling out to Ash.

"Ash Williamson, how dare you not call me? I had to find out second-hand from Hope, who had to hear it from Chase." When she spots Breanna, she lets go of my hand. I have to shake my fingers out to return the blood flow. She rushes over to the couch, where Breanna is sitting with a newborn baby. "Oh my gosh, look at her." Her voice softens as she squishes herself next to them. "She's so bloody perfect. Can I hold her?" Lily's eyes shift to Breanna, and I can tell that she's not handing that baby over to anyone.

Breanna turns to Ash, like he can answer Lily's question. Those two are so fucking in tune with each other. It doesn't take Ash longer than thirty seconds to change Lily's focus from wanting to hold the baby back to him.

"What the hell are you doing here, Lil?" Ash grumbles, taking the infant from Breanna.

"Well, it's not every day that you become a second cousin. Did you expect me not to come? And you're welcome, by the way. Well, really, you should be thanking Alex."

Breanna's face goes blank. I've seen that same expression when she's playing poker, and it's never good—it means she's plotting something. "What are we thanking Alex for?" She directs her question to me.

"You don't need to thank me for anything, Breanna. I just had a baby capsule seat installed in a couple of your cars in the basement." I shrug.

"How the fuck did you get into my cars?" Ash grunts.

I raise my eyebrow, giving him a "bitch, please" kind of look. Breanna rolls her eyes at me—she's obviously not impressed. Ash just laughs and shakes his head.

"Thank you. I almost feel bad that I called them now." Ash pulls his phone out when it starts vibrating. He ignores the notification and returns the device to his pocket.

"Who'd you call?" Lily asks, her eyebrows drawn down in confusion.

"Huh? Oh, don't worry, you're about to find out in: three, two, one." The lift doors open, and in walk four large men.

"I'm going to bloody smother you in your sleep, Ash Williamson," Lily grits out before turning her smile on our... guests.

"Theo, Aunt Holly didn't mention you were in town." She calmly walks up and hugs him, kissing him on both cheeks. I grind my back molars so fucking hard I'm surprised I don't feel a tooth break. Who the fuck is she kissing?

"That's because she doesn't know we're here," the guy responds.

"Ah, actually, she does now," another says, answering his phone and walking off in the direction of the kitchen.

My hands clench as I watch the remaining two men take turns hugging and kissing Lily on her cheeks. I'm about to take a step towards them when Breanna stops me. Holding my arm, she whispers, "They're her cousins on her mother's side of the family."

I give her a thankful look before I pull the mask firmly back into place. Thank God I didn't go apeshit on her fucking cousins. How many fucking cousins does one girl bloody need anyway?

"So, I guess I can't cut their fingers off then?" I ask Breanna.

"Yeah, definitely not these ones," she murmurs. I'm confused by her statement as I watch her approach the men.

"Theo, it's been way too fucking long." Breanna hugs him.

"Breanna fucking McKinley, the pictures really do you no justice." He rakes his eyes up and down her body, showing an indecent level of interest. His perusal's completely different from how he looked over Lily.

"Why thank you. You haven't grown into as much of an ogre as I expected." Breanna laughs.

I notice Lily is purposely keeping her distance from me. *Interesting.* I'm too curious as to what's going on in her head to make a move. She's nervous, that much I can tell. But why?

"I heard you were shacked up with Ash. No one mentioned you went and had a baby. Did I miss the wedding?" Theo asks Breanna.

"No, you haven't missed it. Come meet Faith." She drags him by the hand, over to where Ash stands, and gestures to the newborn.

"Lil Pill, I didn't know you were dropping by." Zac walks back out with Josh.

"Uncle Zac, thank God you're here." Lily huffs out a breath. "Alex and I got those baby seats you guys wanted; they're in the cars."

"Hold the fuck up, buttercup." The other brother comes storming back into the room. I'm reaching for my gun when Zac stops him with a hand on his chest.

"Matteo, you'll be best to remember that my granddaughter is in this room. Save your bloodshed for another day," Zac grunts before letting him go.

"Don't worry, Uncle Zac, there won't be any bloodshed here. We're not heathens. We bought a warehouse for that." One of the younger men smirks.

"TMI, Luca." Josh walks over, positioning himself next to Breanna in a protective stance. *Weird.* Does he see these men as a threat?

"Lily, care to introduce us to your... friend?" Theo asks, looking me up and down with... disgust?

"You know I would, but we really got to go. Things to do. People to see. Tell Aunt Holly I said hi." Lily takes my hand and drags me towards the lift. I willingly follow her, although I'd love to teach the fucker a lesson and knock him down a peg. Who the fuck does he think he's looking at? He's Lily's cousin. I can't maim Lily's family. But fuck, it'd feel good if I could.

The younger two brothers are both standing in front of the doors, blocking her ability to enter the lift. I look between them. They need to fucking move. A growl leaves my chest. Lily squeezes my hand and shakes her head no.

"Ash, here's everything you need." Alyssa walks into the room, surveying the crowd of onlookers. "Oh, for goodness' sake, no. *This* is not happening right now. However, you four boys turned up at the right time. Come and help me move all this stuff into the bedroom." She gestures to the heaps of baby supplies strewn across the floor and furniture.

"Ah, sure, Luca and Romeo will help you, Aunt Lyssa. Matteo and I are going to walk Lily out to her car," Theo says.

Like fuck are they walking Lily anywhere. Cousins or not, I will slit the fucking throats of anyone who gets in my way.

"Great. Ash, here's the bag; everything you should need is in here. Are you sure you don't want me to come with you?" Alyssa asks. He and Breanna must be taking the baby out for the first time.

"Thanks, Mum. We're good. We won't be long." She passes him the bag, and he hangs it over his shoulder.

"Ah, Alex, think you can show us how these car seats work?" Ash walks towards the lift and presses the button. "Sorry, Theo, you'll have to save your fun for another day."

"That's okay. We'll be sticking around for a bit." Theo smirks, looking directly at me. I send him a glare rivalling his own.

"Wait, how long is a bit?" Lily asks.

The fact she has yet to introduce me to her cousins doesn't go unnoticed. I won't call her out on it in front of an audience though. I'll wait until we're in the car, and then I'll find out what the fuck is going through her head.

"As long as it takes," Matteo says. I'm picking up on the names as each of the boys are addressed.

"Great... Oh, did anyone tell you Hope's been trying to get this one's best mate, Chase, into bed?" Lily smirks at Ash.

"Trying and succeeding are two different things, Lil. Chase doesn't have a death wish." Ash looks to Theo.

"Matteo, call the car around. I think we have another cousin to pay a visit to today," Theo commands.

"Theo, no. Chase is family." Ash steps into the lift.

Lily is quick to pull me in, before she presses the buttons to close the door.

"See you around, boys." Lily smiles and waves as the door shuts on them. The moment the lift starts descending, her body slumps into mine. She then turns her glare on Ash. "What the hell did you call him for, Ash? Really, that's dirty even for you," she seethes.

"What's wrong? Not happy to see your cousins, Lil? I know I'm your fav, but still, they *are* family." Ash shrugs.

"You are my least favourite cousin right now."

"Anyone want to fill me in on what the hell that was?" I look to each of them for answers.

"That was Ash being a bloody gossip and not keeping his mouth shut," Lily growls. "Don't worry, I'm calling Aunt Holly. She will tell them they can't touch you."

"Can't touch me? Lil, I don't need your aunt to protect me from your cousins." I laugh.

"Eh, you just might," Ash suggests.

"Why?"

"Wait, you don't know who they are? Here I was, thinking everyone knew of the great Theo Valentino," Breanna says.

Lily's related to the fucking mafia? What the actual fuck? Why didn't she think that was information she should have shared with me by now? I do my best to school my features. I can feel their eyes on me.

After helping Ash navigate the use of a baby seat, I

lead Lily to our own car. Opening the passenger door, I wait for her to get in. She looks at me, trying to gauge how I'm feeling about finding out my girlfriend's family is the goddamn mafia. I don't give anything away. Silently, I nod my head towards the seat, begging her to just get in the fucking car.

Once I'm positioned behind the wheel, I start the engine, and the tyres spin as I peel out of the underground garage. I exhale, trying to compose myself, so that I can have a conversation with her without losing my shit.

19

Lily

'm going to kill Ash. Why the hell would he call and blab to Theo? What did he think it would achieve? *Asshole.* I bet he enjoyed watching me squirm, while stuck in his apartment with my four bloody mobster cousins and Alex.

Sitting in the car heading back to Alex's house, I note how closed-off he is. I can tell he's not happy. His fingers are gripping the wheel so hard his knuckles are white.

"You can just drop me at my house if you want," I offer quietly. I don't expect him to stay interested in dating me, now that he knows who my cousins are. I'm sure he doesn't have a death wish. I don't think they'd really kill him—well, hopefully they wouldn't. I actually don't *know* what they'd do. They didn't look like they wanted to play nice and have a dinner party while welcoming Alex into my life.

"Fuck no! I'm not dropping you anywhere. We're going home. To our home, Lily," Alex grunts.

"*Your* home. I haven't moved in." *Shit... not the time to argue semantics, Lily.* The look Alex sends me is one he usually saves for those he's thinking about maiming.

"Deny it all you want, but you haven't slept a night out of my fucking bed since the day we met. That makes it *our* home. Do you think I'd just bring any woman into my home? Around my family?" He doesn't give me time to answer his question before he continues. "No, I fucking wouldn't. I've been more honest with you than I have with anyone else. I've told you shit I should never have told another soul. And all this time, you've been hiding a big fucking secret from me." He inhales and exhales slowly. "Why, Lily? Why would you not tell me that your family is the fucking mafia?" he asks in a much quieter voice.

"I-I didn't want to scare you away. I don't want to

lose you, okay? It's one thing for you to accept the craziness that is my dad's side of the family, but my Aunt Holly... She's my mum's twin sister. She married Uncle T when she met him in New York. I'm sorry... I get it if you don't want to have anything to do with me anymore."

"Uncle T? Lily, you literally call the fucking Don of the Valentino organization... *Uncle T*. Jesus Christ." Alex shakes his head. "Get this through your pretty, little, stubborn fucking head. Lily, I'm never going to let you go. I don't care if you tell me you're blood cousins with Hannibal Lecter. You could literally be the spawn of the devil himself, Lily. There is nothing in this world that will make me give you up."

"Thank you..." I whisper. Alex curses as he peers in the rear-view mirror. Looking behind me, I see a blacked-out SUV following us. "Is that one of your cars?" I ask him.

"Nope." I pull out my phone and dial the one person I know will force my cousins into line. Hopefully... "Who are you calling?" Alex asks.

I hold up a finger to tell him to be quiet.

"Lily, sweetheart, what a pleasure. How are you?" my uncle answers.

"I'm good, Uncle T. How's my favourite uncle? Did you get those cookies I sent you?" I plaster on the sweetest voice I can muster. Uncle T has a huge soft spot for Hope and me. He always wanted a daughter but got four boys instead.

"I sure did. They were amazing. You really should have gone to culinary school, instead of swimming with the sharks." He laughs.

"Thanks, but I like the sharks. Hey, Uncle T, do you think you can call off the cars your jackass sons currently have following me?"

"What did those idiots do now?" Not even a minute later, I watch as the SUV swerves and makes a sharp U-turn.

"They're trying to intimidate my boyfriend. I really like this one, and he's sticking no matter what they say."

"Boyfriend, huh? This boyfriend got a name?"

"He does."

"Care to give it to me?" He laughs.

"Depends... What are you going to do with it?" I counter.

"Lily, you don't need to give me Alessandro's name, but I'd appreciate it more coming from you. I've called off your tail, and I'll speak to your cousins. *But* you need to be careful. Make sure this is the path you really want to be on, sweetheart. This life isn't for everyone."

"I know, but I—" I stop... I was about to tell my uncle that I love Alex. I don't think that's something I need to share with the world just yet.

"I'm sure you do, but love does not conquer all. Not in our world."

"Thanks, Uncle T. Tell Aunt Holly I said hi." I hang up before he questions me further.

Alex looks over at me. "Lily, I don't need you to call your uncle. If they want to follow us around, let them. I won't ever back down from a fight when you're the prize."

"I don't want you to have to fight, Alex. I want you to be safe and stay in one piece. I happen to be very fond of that body you have going on. I'd hate for anything to happen to it."

"Nothing will happen to me." Alex sounds so confident. He picks up my hand and threads his fingers with mine. "You worry too much. I don't like it."

"People tend to worry about those they care about, Alex."

"If you care about my wellbeing so much, then maybe you should move in with me, you know, so you can keep an eye on me at all times." The smile he gives me lights up his whole face.

"Me, moving in with you, before we're married, is not a good idea. Some of my family's very... traditional." I smile.

"Right, well, let's fix that. Let's get married."

"You can't be serious." I stare at him. "Holy shit, you're serious."

"As a heart attack." How do I respond to that? He's crazy if he thinks we should get married. He's been saying that since the day we met. Maybe what my dad told me is true... *When you know, you just know.* But marriage? "Don't worry, babe, we have all the time in the world. I'll keep asking you every day until you want to say yes."

"I already want to say yes, Alex." The words slip free without thinking.

"That's as good as a yes to me." He smiles. "I fucking love everything about you, Lily Williamson. I can't wait to make you Lily Mancini."

"Who said I'd take your name?"

"You will," he answers. *Cocky asshole.* I happen to be very traditional and would gladly take the name of my husband. But I'd like to make him sweat a little.

"It's the twenty-first century, Alex. I'm not changing my name."

"Lily, you have to. It would be the biggest *fuck you* and extremely disrespectful to me if you didn't. What will the men under me think if my own wife doesn't want my name?"

I didn't consider that perspective. "Guess we'll have to stay living in sin then. In separate homes, of course."

"Fucking hell." Alex does the whole breathing slow thing again. "If it's that important to you, then I'll figure it out," he says eventually. This man is willing to move heaven and earth to marry me. He would willingly face the shame of his wife not taking his name. Not that I think it's shameful, but those in his world would.

"Alex, pull over."

He glances in my direction, then swerves onto a side street. Before the car's stopped, I have my seat belt off and I'm climbing over the centre console to straddle him.

"What are you...?" His question goes unanswered when I claim his mouth with my own. He doesn't put up a fight as my hands travel down his pecs, across the firmness of his abs, until I get to his waistband. I undo his belt, then his button and fly. I have his hard cock in my hands.

I love the feel of his cock. The skin is smooth, silky, hard and soft at the same time. Curling my fingers around the base, I pump up and down, twisting my hand around the tip.

"I fucking love you, Alex Mancini. Let's get married. *Now.* I want to be your wife. I want to take your name. I want you today. I want you tomorrow. I want you always."

Alex lifts my skirt up around my waist. He pulls my panties aside, lining up his cock with my entrance before slamming my hips down.

"I'd marry you in a heartbeat, Lily, but what about your family?" I freeze. *Has he changed his mind? Is my family too much for him?* Fuck, he can't do this to me. He can't make me want him, to the point I can't think straight, then pull the rug out from under me. "I'm not changing my mind," he says, as if reading my thoughts. "That's not what I meant. I meant wouldn't you want your family to be there when you get married? I don't want you to give up your dream wedding for me."

"My dream wedding is marrying you. That's all. But

you're right. We shouldn't do this without my sister or my parents," I admit. I really would love for them to be there.

"That's all you need? Not the rest of the tribe?"

"No, I don't want anyone else there. This is about us, not the world."

Speaking of Hope, her ringtone "Hey Sister"—which she set for herself on my phone—starts blaring from my bag. I ignore it, and instead, I focus on Alex. I'm currently impaled on his cock, and he hasn't moved. I circle my hips; the rumble of his groan vibrates through his body.

The phone starts up again straight away. "Damn it, hold that thought."

I dig through my bag. Alex groans as I practice my pelvic floor exercises while he's inside me. "What the hell are you doing to me?" he grunts.

Laughing, I answer the call. "Hope, I'm a little busy. Is it important?"

"What are you doing right now, Lily? I got this weird feeling that something big was happening."

Oh shit... My eyes widen. The curse of being a twin, she always bloody knows. "Ah, you have to promise not to tell anyone."

"Promise. Now spill. What's happening."

"Okay, Alex asked me to marry him. I said yes."

The shrill of her scream makes me pull the receiver away from my ear.

"What the fuck, Lily Hope Williamson! Why didn't

you call me already?"

"Because, Hope Lily Williamson, it only just happened. And right now, I have my fiancé's dick buried deep inside my vagina. So, if you don't need anything else, I'm going to go and finish what I started."

"Ew, gross. Have fun. Call me as soon as you're done. I want details, Lil." Hope hangs up, and I toss the phone onto the passenger's seat.

"Now, where were we?" I ask Alex.

"Say it again," he growls as he thrusts upwards, his cock hitting that sweet spot.

"Say what?"

"Fiancé. Say it again," he demands.

"I fucking love having my fiancé's dick inside me."

"I can't wait to call you my wife. Once we're finished here, call your parents and have them cancel any plans they have tomorrow. We're getting married."

"Let's not talk about my parents while you're fucking me—it's weird," I pant, while grinding my clit against his pelvis.

"Deal. Who's about to make you come, Lily? Whose cock is your hungry little pussy choking right now?"

"Yours!"

"Wrong answer. Whose is it, Lily?"

"Ah, God, My fiancé's!" I scream as I come, and my eyes roll back into my head. Alex tenses beneath me as his thrusts become rigid spurts of warm liquid coating my insides.

20

I'm sitting in my office, and a shocked Leo is occupying the chair across from me. "Are you sure, Alex? It's been a week?"

"I've never been more sure of anything in my life," I answer honestly.

"Okay, well, what do you need me to do?"

"We're going to need increased security for a while.

Lily's cousins are in town, and I don't trust those fuckers one bit. I don't want anyone getting in the way, or trying to put a stop to this."

"Who are her cousins?" Leo asks.

"Theo Valentino's boys." I don't need to explain who he is. Everyone has heard of the Valentino family.

"What the actual fuck? How did we not know this? How is that even possible? She's not even Italian."

"Her mother's twin sister is the wife of the Don," I answer.

"Holy shit."

"Holy shit indeed."

"Do you think they're responsible for blowing up the beach house?" Leo questions. We still haven't found the asshole behind that. There's also the mystery of who the fuck has those photos of Lily from the night at the beach.

"No, I don't think so. But I'd like to fucking put all that shit to bed. Whoever it is has been quiet. I'm sure we'll find out who the fuck they are and what they want soon enough."

"Well, they want what everyone wants. What you have, your spot."

"They can keep wanting."

"So, have you told Mia about these plans for tonight?"

"Told me what?" Speak of the devil, and she'll appear.

"Your brother is putting a ring on it. Tonight, apparently." Leo smirks at me. I get he doesn't agree with what he sees as a rushed trip down the aisle. But I don't fucking care what anyone says.

"What?" Mia looks at me in shock.

"Tonight, Lily and I will be married. I'll have a car ready to escort you and Tessie. Leo, you'll ride with them."

"Wait, are we not going to discuss this? Like, at all?" Mia questions.

"It's not up for discussion. I asked; she said yes. We're getting married. I would appreciate you not fighting me on this, Mia. I want this. I want her."

"Okay, if you're sure. At least she's not a ditzy bimbo, I guess."

"Thank God, I was worried for a moment you'd never meet anyone worthy," Leo grumbles.

"Not that I was seeking either of your approvals, but thank you."

I leave them in my office and head upstairs. Hope has had Lily locked in the bedroom all morning, with some crap about spending their last day of freedom doing sister shit.

Well, I'm done being shut out. I'm craving Lily. I'm just about to the door when my phone vibrates in my pocket. "Yeah?" I answer without looking at the screen.

"Alessandro, I have something for you. But if you want it alive, you should probably get here in the next twenty minutes. I'll send you the address." Josh's voice is gruff. He ends the call without another word.

Fuck! I dial Leo. "Yeah?" he says through the receiver.

"Get a car ready. Josh has something for us." I hang up and school my features before I enter the room. I'm not leaving this fucking house before I get a taste of Lily.

Opening the door, I find Hope and Lily sprawled across the bed, an arrangement of snacks laid out around them.

"You're missing a vagina, Alex. You weren't invited." Hope laughs at her own joke.

"Thank God he's missing a vagina, because his cock is just soooo good." Lily giggles. Great! Now that cock wants to come out and play with her.

"As much as I love hearing how much you love my cock, babe, I can't stay. I just came in to tell you I'm heading out for a bit. I'll see you tonight though. There will be a driver downstairs, waiting to take you both to the place I've booked."

"Can't you give me a little hint as to where it is?" Lily whines.

"Nope."

"What about me? You can tell me. I can keep a secret?" Hope tries.

"From her? I doubt it."

They both laugh at that. I swoop down and pick

Lily up, carrying her through the bathroom and shutting the door.

"What are you...? Ohhh, did you miss me?" Lily asks when she feels just how hard my cock is.

"I always miss you, babe. I just need a quick taste to tide me over until tonight," I whisper while trailing my lips up the side of her neck.

"Alex, where are you going?"

"I can't tell you that."

"Will you be safe?" She holds my face in her hands, searching my eyes.

"Yes. I'll be fine. It's just business, Lily. Don't worry about me."

"I don't think I can *not* worry about you. Every time you walk out that door, I'm going to worry you won't come back. But I'd have the same worry no matter what job you had. It's not your choice in profession that makes me worry. Well, maybe a little, but mostly it's the thought of you not coming back to me... It terrifies me."

"I will always come back to you, Lily. I promise. Now, give me those lips, so I at least have something pleasant to taste for the next few hours."

She does just that; she brings her lips down softly onto mine. "I love you, Alessandro Mancini," she whispers into my mouth.

"I love you, Lily Williamson."

"Did he say who it was?" Leo asks—for the tenth time—as we get out of the car at the address Josh sent me.

"No, but I'm sure we're about to find out."

We've arrived at a deserted old factory by the docks. This place has always given me the fucking creeps. The chill in the air. The dark corners anyone can jump out of. The odour of rotting marine life. None of it bodes well.

The door of the warehouse is open when we get there. Leo instructs the twenty guys we brought with us to surround the building, while he and I enter.

"Are those...? They fucking are... they're pigs, Alex. I've heard the rumours about this crazy bastard and his pigs." Leo shutters.

"They're all true. You'd be wise to keep that in mind." Josh steps out of the shadows, right in front of us.

"Fucking hell, was that necessary?" I ask, lowering the barrel I have aimed in his direction.

The crazy fucker just laughs. "*I* thought so. Come on. There're two of them."

"Where'd you find them?" I question. My men have been scouring the streets nonstop for the assholes who blew up my fucking house.

Josh ignores my question as he pushes through a door. The room is dark, damp, and fucking reeks of rotting flesh, piss, and shit. There's one fluorescent lightbulb flickering from the ceiling, and two men currently tied up to... crosses? *Okay, that's fucking weird.*

"What's with the crosses?" I ask, not taking my eyes off the fuckers.

"Found them in a church. Thought it was fitting." Josh smirks.

I make the sign of the cross over my body. I may not be the best Catholic, but this is too much even for me. "You know you're going straight to hell, right?" I look at Josh.

"Nope, Emmy's going to heaven. I'll blow the pearly gates down to get to her. Not even God himself can keep me away."

"Yeah, not sure that's how it works. But good plan. Maybe keep the gates open for me then."

Leo makes himself comfortable as he watches. He's always the quiet one, the one who observes from a distance until he's needed. That's why we work so damn well together. He always knows just when to step in.

Walking around the makeshift crucifixes, I look the men up and down, while folding the sleeves of my shirt to my elbows. I stop directly in front of them, staring each in the eyes—one at a time—although theirs are both bruised and swollen.

"Let me introduce myself. My name is Alessandro Mancini. Perhaps you've heard of me?" They knew who I was the minute I stepped into the room. I saw the recognition mixed with fear in their eyes. "If you have a weak stomach, this is the part where you step out." I tell Josh, though the statement is more for these assholes than it is for his benefit.

"I'm good," Josh says, sitting on a chair in the corner of the room.

"Leo, bag." I wait for him to bring it to me. He drops the bag at my feet and immediately returns to his spot by the door. He leans casually against the wall. I open the bag and pull out the instruments, one by one, holding them up before laying them out on the floor in a line. "There are ten instruments here. Most men don't make it past the second. Let's see how far you get," I say to the guy on the right, the one with the most defiant look in his eyes. I'll break him first.

"Fuck you, Mancini." He spits at me. *The dirty fucker.*

"No thanks. You're not my type. Besides, my fiancée would do worse than I ever could. She's the jealous sort." At the word *fiancée*, Josh grumbles. He doesn't say anything audibly though. Now is not the time. "Step one. These little pliers, they look innocent. How much pain could they possibly inflict?" I walk around my intended target, examining his body before I pinch a piece of his flesh between the jaws, which are sharper than any butcher's knife. The fucker screams and howls.

"You see, most people assume I'd use these to rip off a fingernail. A toenail maybe? Nope, I like to slowly, inch by inch, tear a little piece of flesh away." I glance over my shoulder as Leo silently drops an empty bucket beside me. "Now, I don't care if it takes me all night to fill this bucket, but fill it, I will," I lie. I've got a fucking wedding to get to. I need these fuckers to break quickly. I won't show them that though. "Who sent you to blow up my house?" I ask, releasing a square of his flesh into the container.

"Fuck you. I'm not talking," he grunts out between gritted teeth. Without a word, I squeeze another bit of flesh alongside his belly button—it hurts the most around the naval. *Or so I'm told.* "Ahh, fucker!" he yells.

Once again, I meticulously deposit my prize and go straight for the next. His upper thigh. Another sensitive part of the body. His screams overshadow the sniffles of the idiot beside him.

"Who sent you?" I ask again, my voice calm. Much calmer than I'm actually feeling, at the moment. The fucker shakes his head no. "Okay, moving on to step two." I drop the pliers and pick up the next instrument in my line: a sanding block. But this one doesn't have regular sandpaper on it—no, with the right amount of pressure, this grit will remove flesh from bone.

I glide the block over the length of his arm, blood

trailing behind as his skin's diminished to human confetti. He passes out. The fucker actually passes out from the pain. Slapping his face, I watch as he comes back. "Who. The. Fuck. Sent. You. To. Blow. Up. My. House!" I scream in his face. My frustration has finally made an appearance.

"It was Bandetto! He paid us five K each. We didn't know it was your house, Alessandro. I swear! We didn't know whose house it was. Let us go." He must see just how unhinged I truly am, because he squeals like the fucking pig he is.

I look over my shoulder to Leo, who already has his phone out barking orders. Bandetto has been a fucking pain in my ass for the last few months. I never would have thought he'd be stupid enough to try to over-throw me though.

"Damn it, I had eight left. They never get past step two." I turn and complain to Josh, who just smirks at me. Pulling my gun out from behind my back, I don't waste time as I put a bullet between one pair of eyes, then the next. *I'm in a hurry, after all.* "I'm assuming those pigs of yours are hungry," I say out loud, as I pack the instruments back into my bag, before straightening and handing everything to Leo.

"Always are," Josh answers.

"Good, I've got a wedding to attend. I'm getting married today." I smile, proud as fuck.

"Does her father know about this?"

"He does." I nod my head as I exit the room.

"Don't fucking hurt her, Alex, or that will be you tied up to one of those crosses," Josh yells to my back. I don't answer him. I just keep walking.

21

I can't believe he did this. Alex booked out the whole Sydney Aquarium. I'm standing here, in front of a huge tropical display, in a white dress. This seems like a dream. How did he do this? I don't even care how. He did it just so he could marry me.

I love this place. I love being with the animals. The fact that he thought of this all on his own tells me how much he really does love me. How much he listens to me when I ramble on. I look around, a sense of peace overcoming me like I've never felt before.

This is meant to be. We are meant to be.

"Lil, if you want, I can get you out? Run while you still can," my dad jokes.

"I don't think there is anywhere else I'd rather be right now, Daddy," I tell him honestly.

"I know, princess. But you know, Jesus is forgiving. It might not be too late for the nunnery."

"It's too late." I laugh.

"So, how'd you manage to get them to shut this place down for you?"

"I didn't. Alex did," I say.

"Impressive."

"I know. I'm pretty sure you're meant to be walking me into the next exhibit, right? Are you ready? Because I'm really, really ready," I admit.

"I'm never going to be ready. Lily, you are my little girl, always will be. Don't ever forget that. And thank you for not running off to Vegas to do this without me."

"Like you and Mum?" I ask.

"Exactly. I've been both dreaming and dreading the day I get to walk you girls down the aisle."

"I know. Do I look okay?" I run my hands down my plain white dress; it ends just above my knees. It's not exactly what my mum would have picked out, but it's perfect for me.

"You look stunning. Shall we?" My dad holds out

his arm. I loop my hand through his elbow, and together we walk into the shark exhibit. This room has a tank going all the way around the circular interior before the glass continues over our heads. It's as close to standing in the middle of the ocean and staying dry as you can get.

My breath catches when I see Alex at the other end of the runner. Damn, he looks good in a tux. When we stop in front of him, my dad shakes his hand before kissing my cheek. My mum and Hope are already crying. Mia and Leo stand next to them with Tessie, who's in a beautiful white princess dress and holding up a pillow with rings on it.

"Are we ready to begin?" the celebrant asks.

"Yes," we answer at the same time.

The rest of the ceremony is a blur. We exchange vows; neither of us prepared anything prewritten. Instead, we just speak from our hearts.

"I now pronounce you man and wife; you may kiss your bride," the celebrant finally says.

Alex picks me up off my feet as he brings his mouth down to mine. "Finally," he huffs, right before our lips join. I forget everyone else is in the room, returning the kiss with as much love and passion as I can.

When he pulls back, I look up and see a huge stingray swim over our heads. It's beautiful. "This is amazing. Thank you for doing this. I can't believe I got married under the sharks. I can't think of a more perfect place."

"You're welcome, Mrs. Mancini." Alex smiles. I return his goofy grin tenfold. I'm now Mrs. Mancini. I have a husband. *Holy shit, we actually did this.* We're interrupted by a heap of people bringing in tables and chairs.

"What are they doing?" I ask.

"They're setting up for dinner. You didn't think I'd marry you and not feed you, did you?"

"We're eating here? Oh my God, Alex, I freaking love you." I scream and jump into his arms again. The clearing of my dad's throat behind us has me pulling back. Shit, I forgot everyone was here.

"Are you my aunty now, Lily?" Tessie asks me.

"Ah?" I look to Mia for an answer. Tessie is her daughter. If she doesn't want her to call me *aunty*, that's up to her.

"Yes, Tessie. Lily is your aunty now." Mia smiles.

"Yes! Does that mean Hope can be my aunty too?" Tessie looks at Hope. "Because they're the same, so Hope should be my aunty too, right?"

"They're not the same, Tessie, trust me. But I'm sure Hope won't mind being called *aunty*," Alex says, bending to pick her up. "Now, let's eat."

Alex pulls my chair out and hands Tessie to Mia, who sits her in her own seat.

"I can't believe you're married before me. I'm going

to be the old spinster twin. I can see it now," Hope grumbles.

"I'm okay with you being an old spinster, princess. You can live with Mum and me forever," Dad offers.

"Great, just how I pictured my life turning out," she grunts.

"Don't be so dramatic, Hope. You're young. You literally have plenty of time," Mum says. "Now, let's toast to Lily and Alex. If you so much as mess up a hair on my daughter's head, I'll make sure no one ever finds your body. I won't even have to do it myself. I have connections."

"Oh my god, Mum! Stop, just no. Besides, Alex already knows about the Valentino side of the family. Did you not see the boys yet? They're in town."

"Wait, Theo's in town? Why the hell am I the last to know everything?" Hope asks.

"Not just Theo. All four of them are here." I shrug.

"And they haven't busted in and dragged you out to lock you in some tower? They must be losing their touch." Hope laughs.

"Nope, I called Uncle T yesterday and told him to pull them in line." I smile.

"Yeah, that's never going to happen," my mum says.

"Mrs. Mancini, are you ready to consummate this union?" Alex smirks down at me. He's standing at the edge of the bed I'm currently naked and sprawled out on.

"So ready." My hand travels down my body. I'm dying to be touched. So desperate, in fact, I'm willing to be the one to do the touching. Alex has been torturing me for the last hour, kissing and licking all over every inch of my body. If I didn't know any better, I'd think he was trying to mark his bloody territory with his tongue and teeth. I've never been covered in so many bite marks before.

"Don't you dare touch it. That pussy belongs to me; it's mine to touch." Alex bats my hand away. He slides one finger ever so lightly through my wet folds. "It's mine to taste." He bends down and glides his tongue from my ass right up to my clit, circling it around. *Again.* And so lightly it's driving me insane. Just as I'm about to take hold of his head and push him against my mound, he straightens. Lining up his cock with my entrance, he says, "It's mine to fuck!" Then he thrusts forward.

"Oh God, yes, Alex. It's yours. Please fuck it," I beg.

"Oh, I plan to, every day for the rest of my fucking life." Alex picks up one of my legs, resting it on his shoulder. He tilts my hips slightly to the side as he thrusts in deeper with the new angle.

His fingers dig into my ankle, before he turns his mouth and bites down on the spot just above his grasp. The pain radiates through me, sending shock waves straight to my core. My walls tighten, quivering as I come. I've never orgasmed as hard as I do when I'm with Alex.

It's as if he can reach inside me and bend my body to his will. He continues to thrust as I ride out my orgasm. My eyes meet his, once I've fallen back down to earth.

"I fucking love watching you come, Lily. It's the most erotic thing I've ever seen."

I can feel the blush rise up from his compliment. I know he means every word; he never says anything for the sake of saying it. But damn, how do I respond to that?

"Then you better work on making me come multiple times a day for the rest of your life, so you can keep seeing it," I challenge him.

"Oh, I plan on it. Hold on," he says as he flips me over onto my hands and knees. He enters me from behind. "I know I should be making love to you, but fuck, you bring out the animal in me, Lily. An animal that wants to fuck you so hard my cock will be forever imprinted on the walls of your pussy."

Oh fuck, his dirty mouth makes me wetter than I was. I'm not even sure how that's possible, because I was already weeping for him. His words always affect me that way though; I can't get enough of them.

"I want you to fuck me like an animal, Alex. Show me what you got." I grind back onto his cock.

"Fuck. You're so fucking perfect. Good girl. Just like that. Grind that pussy on my cock, Lily, like the dirty little girl you are. Fuck!" Alex growls as he slams into me. I meet him thrust for thrust, until my body seizes up. I squeeze my eyes shut. *Stars.* I see stars as I come, and I feel Alex empty himself into me.

I must have blacked out because when I come to, I'm under the covers, wrapped up in Alex's arms.

"Welcome back, babe." He smirks with a proud gleam in his eyes.

"Ah, what happened?"

"I fucked you so hard you passed out. You're welcome, by the way."

"Don't be so smug. How do you know that hasn't happened to me before?"

Oh shit, wrong thing to say, Lily. Wrong thing to say. I literally see the dark shadow that covers Alex's eyes, his jaw clenching.

"How's that list coming along. I'm going to need it real soon," he grits out.

"Ah, what list? You know what? I can't. I don't remember anyone other than you."

"Mmhmm, I'll find out anyway," he murmurs as he kisses my forehead.

"I can't believe we're married." I hold up my hand, my ring staring back at me. "It's so perfect. You are so perfect."

"I'm not perfect, far from it. But you are a fucking angel, an angel who's in bed with the devil. But still an angel I'll worship forever."

"I don't need you to worship me, Alex, just to love me. I just need you to love me. I'm not perfect either."

"Well, to me, you're perfect. If anyone tries to say otherwise, I'll cut their tongues right out of their mouths for speaking such blasphemy."

22

Alex

It's been one week, one week of wedded bliss. Marrying Lily was the best thing I've ever done. We've barely spent any time apart. The only reason I've been in my office without her the last few hours is because I've yet to get my hands on that Bandetto bastard. He's gone fucking underground. But Leo is working on narrowing down the fucker's connection to the Houghten Group and my missing cargo, while I try to hone in on his physical location.

No matter how many men I have scouring the streets, they all come back fucking empty-handed. I can't let Lily out of my sight without knowing where this fucker is. I won't put her at risk. I don't know what the asshole is capable of. Unlike me, he has no fucking morals, and I wouldn't put it past him to use Lily to get to me.

A knock breaks my attention away from my computer screen. I close out the windows as Lily walks through the door. "Hey, babe, come to distract me? Because I welcome that distraction."

"Ah, no, sorry. Breanna's on the line—she's asking for you." She holds the phone out to me.

"Okay. Babe, could you get me a bottle of water from the kitchen, please?" I look to Lily. She glances at the bar fridge in my office before agreeing, leaving the room, and shutting the door behind her. That was too easy. The thing with Lily is she won't ever say anything to contradict me until we're in private. But you can guarantee that once there are no other ears around, she'll gladly let me know what she thinks of me sending her out of the room to take this call. "Miss McKinley, what can I do for you?" I say into the receiver.

There's a long, silent pause before her quiet voice comes through. "I need a favour?"

"People who call me usually do. I would appreciate

it if you don't go through Lily to get to me again." I know my tone is harsh. I'm pissed that she used Lily like that.

"Look, I wouldn't ever ask you for anything. But this... I—Faith has been kidnapped and I'm going to get her back. I don't need your help, but I would appreciate it."

"What happened? Who took her?" I pick up my keys and wallet.

"Her birth mother took her from the hospital today, left a note for Ash asking for five million if he wants her back." I know she's not calling me for a loan. She's a McKinley; she has an abundance of cash at her disposal.

"Okay, what do you need me to do? I'm pretty sure it's not to front the five mil."

"I need you to meet me at my Uncle Dean's. I know where she is. I just need backup, in case she's not alone."

"Okay, I'll be there as soon as I can."

"Also, you can't tell Lily. Ash doesn't know I'm doing this. And I need to keep it that way until after."

"I'm not lying to Lily for you, Breanna. If she asks, I will tell her," I growl into the phone.

"I'm not asking you to lie. I'm asking you to stall for a few hours."

"Okay, I'll see what I can do. I'll meet you at your uncle's."

I pass Lily in the hall as I'm walking out. I grab the

bottle of water out of her hand. "Thanks, babe. Something's come up and I gotta head out for a bit. I need you to stay here until I get back, okay?"

"What happened? What did Bree want?" she questions, stepping in front of me.

"Lily, I promise you everything will be fine." I huff out a breath. I shouldn't tell her, but fuck, how can I not? "If I tell you this, you have to promise me you will stay here and not reach out to Ash until after I get back."

Lily nods her head. "Okay, I promise."

"Faith was taken from the hospital by her birth mother. Breanna called asking for help. I think she's on a one-woman mission to get Faith back."

"Oh my god, Ash doesn't know what she's doing, does he? Damn it, Alex. How can I not call him?"

"Because you just promised me you wouldn't. We don't break promises to each other, Lily. We come first. You and me, above anyone else, babe. Don't forget that." I kiss her forehead before heading for the front door. "Don't leave the house," I call out to her, closing the door behind me.

Leo's waiting for me at the car. I swear the fucker is always ready. I only just sent him a message two minutes ago.

"It's like you have fucking vamp speed." I laugh.

"It's weird as fuck you even know what that is."

"Mia was obsessed with vampire shows as a teen. How could I not know?"

After fifteen minutes, we pull into the McKinley Estate. We're greeted by a butler, then shown through the house and led to the basement. If it weren't for the opulence of our surroundings, it would seem like a fucking bad horror film, where the killer lowers your defences before luring you downstairs. But this isn't your ordinary basement—it's a fucking indoor shooting range.

Just as I'm walking through the door, I hear Theo ask about Ash.

"I'd also like to know why you're coming up with this plan without him?" I grunt. This is his kid. *Why the fuck is his girlfriend out looking for the infant? And not him?*

"What the fuck are you doing here?" Theo turns that icy glare on our entrance.

"You're either fucking stupid as fuck, or have balls of steel," Matteo says to me.

I look at Leo and smirk, before facing Theo and Matteo as I shrug one shoulder. "Funny, your cousin happens to love my balls."

Theo draws a gun from behind his back and aims it straight at my head. Neither Leo or I flinch. As much as he wants to shoot me, I know he won't. *At least, I'm pretty sure he won't.*

"Okay, that's enough. We all know you guys aren't going to shoot each other. Lily would never forgive any of you," Breanna huffs.

"It's a risk I'm willing to take," Matteo says.

"No, you're not. You either need to put your differences aside and help me get my fucking daughter. Or you can all go crawl back to the holes you came from, and I'll do it the fuck alone."

"Where's Ash, Breanna?" Theo asks again.

"I left him at the hospital; he's with his family."

"And he's okay with you going rogue? Going off on your own to get his daughter back?"

I ask her.

"He doesn't know, and she's my daughter too now, so are you helping or not?" she retorts.

"I'm helping, but I do want to know why you're leaving Ash out of this?" I question before adding, "Or should I just call and ask him myself?"

"No, you can't call him. He already has charges against him. I'm not about to let him get himself into any more trouble."

"What charges?" This comes from Matteo; however, Leo is already tapping away at his phone hacking into the police files.

"Ah, just assault charges from a fight he was in a few weeks back." Breanna tries to shrug it off.

"Hey, Breanna?" Leo looks up from his phone, before passing it to me. "Why were Lily and Hope arrested that same night?" he asks. *What the fuck? Lily was arrested?*

"What? How the hell can you even know that already?" Breanna looks shocked.

"Lily and Hope were arrested? What the fuck for?" Theo and Matteo both question at the same time.

"Says here: for assaulting a police officer. What happened that night, Breanna?" I ask, not hiding the fact that I'm fucking proud as shit. I know those girls can fight, but I never thought they'd be the type to fight a cop.

"Ash beat the shit out of some guy who hit Lily at the club. The girls were trying to get to him when the cops were taking him away in cuffs. One stepped in front of Hope, who slapped him across the face, then Lily dropped the officer to the ground."

I see red. Rage like I've never known consumes me. Someone hit Lily? Some cocksucker actually laid their hands on my Lily? I'm going to have fun fucking killing that bastard.

"Who the fuck put their hands on Lily?" I seethe. I pass the phone back to Leo. "I want a name. Now."

"I don't know his name. Last I heard, he was still in the ICU after the beating Ash gave him." Breanna smiles. "Okay, now that that's sorted, get strapped up. We're going to get my daughter back," she commands.

I look to Leo; he knows exactly what I want to do. He nods his head. "I've got the name; we'll deal with it after we get the child back. Trust me, he ain't goin' anywhere," he assures me.

"How do you know where she is?" Matteo asks, referring to the kidnapped infant.

"My dad gave her a bracelet with a GPS tracker

hidden in the little gemstone. The location of that bracelet hasn't moved in the last hour," Breanna explains.

Of course Josh would put a fucking GPS tracker on a human. Although, the more I think about it, the better the idea sounds. I could hide a small tracker in Lily's engagement ring. She'd never have to know, though I'd probably tell her anyway. I can't seem to keep my fucking mouth shut around her.

"Well, that was fucking easier than I thought it would be. You'd think if you were kidnapping and holding a baby ransom for five mil, you'd at least have a bit of security. Maybe someone else helping you out?" Leo says from the passenger side of the car.

I'm breaking every speed limit and road rule there is, my mind solely focused on getting my hands on the fucker who's currently lying in a hospital bed. The one who thought he could put his hands on Lily. I don't care that I didn't even know her when it happened. I know her now, and no one is going to live to tell the story of when they assaulted my fucking wife.

"Yeah, thank fuck it was easy. I don't have time for this shit today," I agree. Getting Breanna and Ash's daughter back was child's play. Breanna could have done that all on her own. When we got to the dilapidated weatherboard cottage, Leo and I went in through the back of the house, while Breanna and the fucking Valentino cousins went in through a side window.

It was Breanna who ended up saving her daughter and walking away without a shed of remorse. I now have a newfound respect for the young McKinley. It seems crazy bloodlust runs in the family.

As we pull into the hospital car park, Leo puts his hand on my arm. I look down at the offending gesture, the one attempting to stop my hasty escape from the car.

"I know you want to go in there, guns blazing and all that. But you need to be smart about this, Alex." When I don't answer him, and instead send him a warning glare, he sighs. "At least let me clear the fucking cameras first."

"You have two minutes," I growl as I sit back in my seat. I just spoke to Lily on the phone not that long ago, but I want to get this done and get back to her. I don't have time to waste.

"I love your blind faith in my tech abilities." Leo's words drip with sarcasm.

"It's not blind faith when I know exactly what you're capable of with that little device of yours." I nod in the direction of the laptop that's not little at all. It's more like a fucking brick. Leo ignores me as he continues to tap away at the keys at an inhuman speed, again making me question his mortality.

A minute later, he smiles as he closes the lid. "Done. Let's do this."

It's not hard to charm my way into the ward where this prick is recovering from the beating Ash gave him. Ash is quickly becoming my favourite of Lily's cousins. I know he's her favourite too; she told me once but swore me to secrecy.

We find the douche sitting up in a hospital bed, his face still sporting yellow and green bruising with dressings wrapped all around his head. His right arm is in a cast. I smile, impressed by Ash more and more by the minute.

I'm at the fucker's bedside before he notices I'm not one of the doctors or nurses he's expecting to see. "Who the fuck are you?" he hisses. *Like the fucker is in a position to do anything other than lie helpless in that bed.*

"Who I am isn't important here. Who *you* are, however, is. Do you know who you are?" I ask him.

"What? Of course I do. Get out of my room."

"No, you don't. But don't worry, I'm going to tell you exactly who the fuck you are," I growl, wrapping my hand around his throat.

"Who am I then, asshole?" He groans through gritted teeth.

"You're the motherfucker, who thought he could get away with laying his filthy fucking hands on my wife." I squeeze, watching as his eyes bulge and his face turns blue. I let go, just before it appears as though he might pass out.

He gasps for breath. "Fuck off. That redheaded bitch didn't have a ring on," he huffs.

I don't hold back with the left hook I throw at his jaw. His head snaps to the side. "That redhead is my wife, motherfucker!" I roar.

"Your what?" This comes from behind me, right about the same time I hear the click of a safety being disengaged. Turning, I come face to face with Theo and Matteo, both of whom are pointing guns in my direction. Leo is on the other side of the bed with his own firearm aimed at them. Fucking hell! Was it too much to expect they wouldn't fucking follow me here?

"My wife. I didn't fucking stutter. Now, if you'll excuse me, I'm in the middle of something." I turn back to the fucker who is staring between me and his two new visitors.

"You see, the problem with that is the *wife* part. I don't recall an invite to any wedding. You get an invite, Matteo?" Theo says, walking towards the bed.

"Nope, must have gotten lost in the mail," Matteo counters.

"You two really want to discuss this right now? Fine, I'll make this quick." I pull out a syringe of morphine. "You know, I'd love to do this another way. In my mind, I see myself skinning you alive, after I remove each of those grubby fingers of yours and shove them up your ass. But it appears my wife's cousins over here are impatient bastards. So, this is going to have to work."

I uncap the tubing on his intravenous drip, slowly administering the morphine. "This is too easy for you, considering the circumstances..." I shrug my shoulders. "But don't worry, I'll be sure to have your body strung up over the Harbour Bridge. You'll serve as a reminder to the rest of the scumbags that my wife is un-fucking-touchable," I hiss, before capping and repositioning his IV. I step back and watch the fucker's eyes drift closed.

This was way too fucking painless for him, and it fucking pisses me off. "Leo, make sure that message gets sent out, will ya?" I glance up when he doesn't answer.

Leo's face is ashen white. He's staring at his phone, then his eyes hesitantly meet mine. And the moment they do, *I know*. Something's wrong... Lily. "No! No, fuck no!" I scream as I walk over to him and snatch the phone out of his hand. I scan the pictures for a few seconds, and relief washes over me before a different kind of dread sets in.

"That's not Lily. That's Hope." I shove the phone back at him and turn to leave, only to have the exit blocked by the fucking Valentino brothers.

"What's Hope?" Theo tilts his head as he inspects my face. They've at least lowered their weapons.

"You can either shoot me or follow me home.

Because I assure you, I'm leaving now. Nothing, not even you, will stop me from getting to my wife." I shoulder barge past them and storm out the door. "Leo, show them the pictures."

I hear them growl in muffled Italian, hissing out what I can only assume are profanities. I don't have time to dwell on whatever the fuck they're saying. I need to get home to Lily. This is going to fucking destroy her.

23

Lily

I told Alex I wouldn't leave, but fuck, I'm going crazy here waiting for him to come back. I've been pacing up and down the foyer, which is no easy feat considering the size of this place. I'm nervous, worried, and fucking annoyed. *All at the same time.* I'm nervous for Alex. What is Breanna getting him involved in? If something happens to him because of her, I don't know if I'll be able to forgive her for dragging him into this mess.

Then... I feel like shit, because of course I want them to get their daughter back. I'm worried about Ash. I want to call him, to go and see him. Despite what I say, he is my favourite cousin. Always has been. I know how worried and stressed he must be right now. I could see how attached he was to that baby. *His baby.*

If it were my child, I'd do anything to get her back.

And lastly, I'm annoyed that I'm left to sit here and twiddle my bloody thumbs. I've never felt more useless. It's been hours. Where the hell is he? Why hasn't he called me yet? Or at least sent a message to let me know he's okay? That Breanna's okay, that they got Faith back, and everything is going to be okay?

My phone vibrates in my hand, and I answer it without looking to see who it is.

"Alex, where the hell are you?" I yell.

"Ah, not Alex, Lil." Hope's voice sounds off... *Something's wrong.* Shit, maybe this unease wasn't about Alex at all... Maybe it's been about my twin the entire time...

"What's wrong, Hope?"

"I'm okay. I'm fine. I just... Can I come and see you?" She sounds upset.

"Of course you can. You don't have to ask. You're welcome here anytime. You know that."

"I love you, Lil."

"I love you too. I'll get the wine chilled," I say, but she already hung up.

Great, now I not only have to worry about Alex, Ash and Bree, but my sister as well. I'd really like my fairy-tale ending to start. I'm ready for the part of my story where it says: *And they all lived happily ever after.*

I'm in my first week of wedded bliss. I should be away on a tropical island somewhere. Not walking around in circles, with the occasional guard looking at me like they're afraid I'm going to lose my mind. I should be sipping cocktails with my extremely hot-ass husband on a beach. Sun, sand, all of that.

Instead, I'm stuck in this house, all because I promised Alex I wouldn't leave. And we don't break promises to each other. That is not the way I want to start our marriage. Giving in, I dial his number. I didn't want to be the needy, clingy wife. *But fuck it.* I am who I am. And if he doesn't like it, well, it's too late. He already put a ring on it.

"Lily, babe, everything okay?" Alex asks when he finally answers the call. I thought it was going to voicemail.

"Ah, yeah. I was just... I was calling to let you know Hope's on her way over," I blabber out.

"Uh, okay. Is she okay?"

"I don't know. I'm sure it's just Hope drama. How's everything going with the business you had to handle?" I ask.

"Good, Breanna and Ash are on their way home with Faith."

"Okay, are you on your way home too?"

"I just have one more stop to make, then I'll be home. Shouldn't take too long."

"Okay, I'll, um... I'll let you go then. Sorry to disturb you."

"Lily, you are not a disturbance. You can call me anytime. I'll always answer, babe. Nothing is more important to me than you."

"Mmm, I love you, Alex. Be safe. I have plans for that vessel you're in tonight. I need it in one piece."

Two hours later, Hope still hasn't shown up and she isn't answering my calls. I don't know what's going on with her, but I have the worst feeling in the pit of my stomach. I can't shake off the dread. But Faith is okay. Breanna and Ash are okay. And Alex is okay. I spoke to him just two hours ago.

A lot can happen in two hours. That negative bitch of a voice says in my head. Fuck, anything—literally anything—can happen in two hours.

I've curled up in the library. I have a bottle of wine in a melted ice bucket with two glasses waiting. I haven't opened it yet, but I should have.

"Lily!" Alex's voice screams out through the house. "Lily, where the fuck are you?" he calls out again.

I jump up and run to the door, just as he's passing through the hall. "I'm right here."

"Oh, thank fuck!" Alex wraps his arms around me so tight I struggle to breathe. He lets go and brings his hands up to my cheeks. Holding my face, he searches my eyes.

"Are you okay? You're fine. You're here. You're okay?" I'm not sure if he's asking, or just trying to reassure himself.

"What happened?"

His face clenches up. He's shutting down like he doesn't want to tell me something. "Did Hope come by?" He changes the subject.

"No, she never turned up. What happened, Alex?" I ask again. Leo walks in with Theo and Matteo trailing behind him. *What the hell?* "Theo, what's going on?" My voice trembles. They're all looking so fucking grim. My pulse quickens, and a cold sweat coats my body.

"Lily, babe, it's going to be okay. I'm going to find her, okay? I'll get her back." Alex takes hold of my hands.

"Get who back? I thought you said you found Faith."

"It's Hope, babe. Somebody has Hope." Alex looks pained as he says it.

It takes a minute for his words to sink in, before they hit, but when they do, I drop to the ground. "No, no, no, no!" I silently shake my head as tears stream down my cheeks.

"Shit, Lily." Alex scoops me up, carrying me back to the library. "It's going to be okay, Lily. I will find her." Alex strokes my hair, but it doesn't matter what he says. He can't promise me it's going to be okay. He doesn't know that.

"I-I can't. Where is she, Alex?" I manage to stutter out. My body is shaking. I can't stop shivering.

"I don't know. I thought... I was sent a photo. Someone claimed they had you, but I knew from the picture it wasn't you."

"Lily, honey, you okay?" Theo asks. I remove myself from Alex's lap, much to his disapproval, and hug my cousin.

"Do you think I'm okay, Theo, really?" I ask as I pull back. Everyone is looking at me. I'm fucking destroyed at the thought of my sister being held by some looney. God knows what's happening to her. She barely survived last time... I can't imagine how she's handling this. "I wish it were me. Why couldn't they have just taken me?" I say aloud. Alex growls behind me.

"We will find her, Lily," Matteo tries to assure me.

Romeo and Luca enter the room. "Why the fuck

are we all standing around here, when we should be out getting our fucking cousin back!" Romeo yells.

"You were too late last time. What makes you think this will be any different?" I ask, and all four of them flinch at the reminder of what happened to Hope when we visited New York one year. I know it wasn't their fault, and I shouldn't be blaming them. *But I'm fucking angry.* I'm fuming. This isn't fair. This can't happen to the same person twice. It's just... not fucking fair. "She's not strong enough," I whisper.

"Yes, she is, and if she isn't, we will be there for her until she is. Leo, have you got anything yet?" Alex looks to Leo.

"Not much. Someone said they heard talk of Bandetto hanging around down at the square. I've sent a few men to look into it. It's like he's a fucking ghost."

"Well, I guess we're the fucking Ghostbusters then, because I'm about to *bust* this motherfucker," Matteo yells.

"Wait, Lily. Do you think your dad is anywhere near as crazy as Josh?" Alex asks me.

"What? No, he's not." I shake my head.

"That necklace with the *L*... Hope has one just like it. You both never take them off. Who gave it to you?" Alex probes.

"Josh did. For our sixteenth birthday. He made us promise not to take them off. *Ever.* And, well, it's Josh. You're better off not defying him." I shrug.

"Fucking Josh. Leo, get him on the phone now," Alex grunts out.

"I don't know if he's a genius or just a plain psychopath." Theo grabs and holds up my necklace, dangling it above my neck.

I bat his hand away. "This has two carats of diamonds, idiot. Don't touch it."

"Two carats? You didn't think it was odd that a man, with no blood relation, gave you and Hope a necklace with two carats of diamonds each? *When you were sixteen*?" Luca asks with his eyes drawn.

"No, it's Josh and Emily. They're always extreme with their gift-giving," I defend them.

"That's true. I'm still trying to find room for all the shit they bought my niece for Christmas a few weeks ago."

"Alex, what's going—*oh, hello.*" Mia walks into the room and stops in her tracks when she spots my cousins.

Theo and Matteo both look at her a little too long. "No! Fucking! Way!" Alex growls.

"Mia, I need you to keep Tessie out of here for a while." Alex stands in front of his sister, blocking everyone's view of her.

"Well, I think you should not be so rude, and introduce me to your new friends." She steps around him.

"Ah, these are my cousins: Theo, Matteo, Romeo and Luca." I point to each.

"How many cousins do you have? And why

couldn't these ones have been here for Christmas?" Mia looks at me. "What happened? Why have you been crying?" At her question, the tears start all over again. She turns to Alex. "What'd you do, idiot?"

"Nothing." He pulls me out of Matteo's embrace and drags me back over to the couch, where he sits me down on his lap. *Again.* He strokes my hair and whispers promises he can't guarantee.

"Someone needs to tell me what the fuck is going on. Now!" Mia stomps her foot.

"I'd be happy to fill you in, sweetheart." Matteo looks her up and down. Leo walks into the room and pulls Mia away from Matteo.

"Josh is on the other line, boss." Leo holds out a phone.

"About bloody time," Alex grunts, snatching the device. "Josh, the tracker you have on Hope, I need her location—*now.*"

24

Alex

Watching Lily fall apart in front of me is shattering my fucking heart. I can't seem to find the right words to comfort her. I've never seen anyone so broken before. I feel fucking helpless, and I don't like feeling fucking helpless.

"And why do I need to track my niece's location, Alessandro?" Josh asks.

"Someone has taken her; they think they have Lily. I need you to track her, so I can go and get her fucking back, Joshua," I growl, using his full name in return.

"What the fuck is wrong with you? I knew you'd be bad fucking news. I swear to God, I'm going to kill you when I get my hands on you, Mancini." I pull the phone away from my ear, Josh's scream ringing out loud enough for everyone else to hear.

"Guess he's a fan of yours." Luca smirks, or maybe it's the Romeo kid? I don't know. They both look the fucking same. If I didn't currently have Lily crying in my arms, I'd get up and knock that smirk off his stupid face. Standing, I hold Lily's slumped body in my arms. I need to get her out of here.

"Let me know when Josh shows," I instruct Leo on my way out of the room.

"Where the fuck do you think you're taking her?" One of the younger Valentino brothers steps in front of me.

Lily flinches, then lifts her head. "Put me down, Alex." Her voice is hoarse from crying.

"I'd rather not," I grunt. I support her until she finds her footing. Once she's able, she turns her glare on her younger cousin.

"Oh boy, you're alone in this one, bro." Matteo laughs.

"Romeo, you might be junior-king shit in your house. But *this*, this is my house, and you're nothing more than a guest. Don't ever speak to my husband like that *under my roof* again." Lily shoves her hands flat against his chest, but he doesn't budge.

"What the hell, Lil? What'd I do?"

"You know what? It doesn't matter. Where's my phone? If y'all are just going to sit here like the dipshits you are, I'll find my sister my damn self. It's me they want anyway. I'll offer them a trade."

"Like fuck you will. Lily, I swear to God, I will lock you in the fucking room if you even think about leaving this house." I bend at the waist and throw her over my shoulder. No one stops my departure this time.

"Alex, put me the fuck down. I'm going to kick your bloody ass." Lily punches my lower back. Again, I'm left wishing she punched like a girl; her jabs actually make a fucking impact.

"Stop hitting me, Lily. Your punches actually fucking hurt." I slap her ass.

"Good. Wait until I put you on your ass again," she yells.

"You know I love your fire, babe. It turns me on. But now is not the time for it." I make a detour and head for the gym, instead of the bedroom.

I put her down in the middle of the room as she pivots towards me. "What are we doing here, Alex?"

"You wanna hit me, Lily, then hit me. You wanna take your frustration out on me, then do it. You wanna blame me for your sister getting taken, you fucking should." My voice sounds calm, but inside I'm dying.

At the end of the day, it is my fucking fault her sister has been abducted by some fucking psychopath asshole. I should have stopped the fucker before he took those pictures of her that night at the beach. I should have left her alone. I should have never let her get close to me. I knew my world would destroy something as pure and perfect as she is. Not even a week after she's taken my last name, and someone has targeted her.

"I don't want to fight you, Alex. What I want to do is leave. I want to find my fucking sister."

"No. I'll literally let you do anything else. You want something? Name it. I'll make sure you have it. The one thing I will never let you do is leave. You can't leave me, Lily. I won't... I can't... You can't leave me." I drop to the floor. Just the thought makes my blood run cold...

"Alex, I'm not leaving you." Lily sits herself in my lap, wrapping her legs around my waist. "I'm never leaving you. I just meant I need to leave this house. I need to get her back, Alex. *I have to.*"

"You're not leaving. I can't protect you outside. I need you to help me by staying put. I will get your sister back. I'm sure Josh will be here any minute now. Once he is, we will go and get her."

"And I just have to sit here?" Lily's eyes widen. "Oh my God, my parents! I have to call my parents." She looks around the room, searching for something.

"Babe, I think maybe we should wait until Josh gets here. Let's go back to the library. You know, if you're still angry, I'll be more than willing to hold down one of your cousins for you to beat on," I offer.

"*Please*, like I'd need you to hold them down. They'd be way too scared to leave a scratch on me. They won't fight back." She laughs as she climbs to her feet. "Come on, we should make sure they're not planting bugs and shit in our house."

"You think your cousins would plant bugs in your home?" I ask her.

"I don't think. *I know.* They bugged our cars when we were sixteen. Theo and Matteo spent a summer with us that year. It took weeks for Hope to figure out how they just happened to know whenever she snuck out to meet boys."

"Just Hope? You didn't sneak out to meet boys?"

"Not until I started university." She smiles.

"So that list, it starts from your uni days. Shouldn't be too long then." I smile.

"You're not getting a list, Alex."

I'll drop it for now, but I'm getting that list eventually. Just as we're walking down the hall, near the library, an angry-looking Josh storms towards us. I shove Lily behind me.

"Don't be an idiot. He's not going to hurt me," Lily hisses, trying to get past me. Josh walks up and throws a right hook my way. I see it coming. I could have ducked, blocked it, but I don't. I revel in the snap of my neck as the hit connects, in the sharp pain that radiates through my jaw. "Oh my God, Josh, stop!" Lily manages to make it around me.

"Lil, I'm sorry, but your piece-of-shit husband is the reason your sister is currently missing. Trust me, one hit is the least he deserves," Josh spits with anger.

"No, Josh, it's not his fault. You need to stop, or leave my house." Lily folds her hands over her chest. Damn, she's hot when she's feisty. Actually, she's hot all the fucking time. Josh turns and starts walking away. *Without a word.* "Wait!" Lily runs up and hugs him. *She fucking hugs him.* I watch as he stiffens at first, but then he returns her embrace. "I'm sorry. I didn't mean that," she whispers, wiping tears from her face. Great, now she's fucking crying again.

"Do you know where she is?" I ask Josh.

"Yep, you have about two minutes to get your shit together. I'm not waiting around for you," he grunts.

"Great, let's go then." Lily starts walking towards the front door.

"Ah, no. Lily, I'm going. You're staying here, where I know you'll be safe." I grab her hand, and lead her and a still-fuming Josh into the library. The four Valentino brothers glare as we enter. "Okay, which one of you is staying here with Lily?" I ask them, watching Theo look from me to his cousin.

"Romeo and Luca will stay with you, Lil. Are we ready to do this?" Theo sends Romeo a look that quickly shuts him up when the kid starts to protest.

"I don't need a damn babysitter, Alex. She's my sister. I'm coming." Lily folds her arms over her chest, which only pops her tits up into my face. I smile, which was not a good move. "Alex, argh, fine! Go. I'll stay here and bake bloody cookies while I wait for the men to be my heroes."

"I'm on a diet. Damn, wish I wasn't. Those cookies of yours are amazing, Lil," Matteo says with one of the best poker faces I've seen. Lily's cookies are anything but good.

"Shut up, Matteo. Go and get my sister back already."

"I'll have my phone on me. Call me whenever you need to, okay?" I kiss her on the forehead and walk out. Josh, the silent fucker, is out front in his blacked-out SUV. I didn't even see him exit the library. He doesn't wait for us to get in our vehicles; he just starts driving. "Fucking ass," I grumble, as I run towards Leo and the passenger seat. Theo and Matteo jump into their own car behind us.

Once we're all piled out onto the road, I notice the convoy of SUVs tailing us. *Subtle*, I think to myself. The fucking mafia. Those aren't my guys; they're Valentino men.

I dial Josh, and surprisingly, he answers. His voice comes over the Bluetooth. "What?"

"Where is she, Josh? Where are we headed, and what are we walking into?" I ask.

"Does it matter? You can back out and go home. I'll get her myself."

"No, it doesn't matter. I want to know what to prepare for though—*that's all.*"

"Honestly, I have no idea. I've tracked her necklace to a house in the Hills District. It's fucking suburbia. Who the fuck knows what's happening? But you might want to keep a better eye on those enemies of yours, Alex. I don't want to be saving my fucking nieces every other weekend."

"Don't worry, I've just sent a message to the whole fucking city. Lily is off-limits. No one will try to touch her again." The fucker hangs up. Doesn't acknowledge my words, just hangs up. Damn it.

"Fucking hell. What if we're too late, Leo? How do I tell Lily? How do I face her parents?" All the worst-case scenarios play out in my head, and they're not fucking pretty. I've seen a lot of sick shit throughout the years. None of it, I want to see happening to my wife's fucking twin sister.

"We can't be. And honestly, you'll probably have to go into hiding if we are. There's no way they'll let you keep Lily if something happens to Hope. That family of hers would close ranks and have her whisked off into an ivory tower, before you could even blink."

"Great, glad I came to you for words of fucking comfort."

"You didn't ask me for comfort. You wanted the truth." We pull up onto a tree-lined street.

"Where the fuck are we?" I question, when we stop at a fucking cookie-cutter McMansion.

"Let's find out." Leo shuts the engine off and we jump out. We approach Josh just as Theo and Matteo, along with their convoy, pull in behind us.

"Well, this should be fun." Josh smirks when he sees the two Valentino brothers and their entourage walking up the street.

"Whose place is this?" I ask. Josh looks suspiciously calm. Something's off...

"You'll see. Remember: shoot first, ask questions later. Any of you fuckers hit Hope, you'll be fucking pig food." He storms up the driveway and kicks in the front door.

Literally kicks in the front door. Way to make a fucking entrance. The house is quiet. And Josh is still being fucking weird. He's navigating the interior like he's been here before. He's not even on high alert as we all blindly follow him up the stairs.

I look behind me to Theo, who is just as puzzled as I am. When we get to a door at the top of the stairs, Josh glances over his shoulder. "Prepare yourselves, boys. What you're about to see can't ever be unseen."

Chills run up my spine. *Fucking hell.* I don't have time to contemplate anything, before Josh is kicking in that door as well. Does the guy not know how to turn a fucking knob?

The graphic scene staring back at me as I enter the room... The shrills and screams that echo off the walls... *This* is not what I was expecting to see. I aim my gun at the fucking idiot's head. Rationally, I know this is Hope, but she fucking looks just like Lily... and nobody wants to see some other fucking scumbag fucking his wife.

25

Lily

It's been five minutes. They left five minutes ago. I need to do something; Romeo and Luca are both watching me like I'm a bloody patient in a mental hospital—*one who's about to snap*. I should have insisted that I went with them. I should have just gone with them. It's my fault Hope's entangled in this mess. I knew Alex's world wasn't safe, and I jumped in headfirst, like a lovesick fool. I can't honestly picture not being in Alex's orbit anymore. I knew the moment I saw him in that shower that he was different.

I knew he was the one. I mean, who marries a man after just a few weeks of dating. *Me, apparently.* Ask me if I regret it? I'd say no every time, because that's the truth. Selfishly, even knowing what's happening now, I'd still marry him. That makes me feel like the shittiest bloody sister of all sisters.

My phone pings with a message.

Josh: Lily, I'm sorry I didn't tell you earlier. Hope is fine. I tracked her location to one of her friend's places. We'll be back with her soon. Don't tell anyone you know this yet. I just couldn't stand knowing you were worried. Your sister's okay.

Me: Which friend?

Josh: One who's about to get scared away. Hopefully.

The relief washes over me instantly. She's okay. She's going to be fine. She's just shacking up with a guy she shouldn't be. That's all. That's okay. Hope is okay. Then it hits me.

Oh shit, Chase. Hope is at Chase's house, and my cousins are about to catch her in the act. Literally. Fuck. I dial Hope's number for the millionth time. It goes straight to voicemail again. Hope will be okay, but I can't say the same thing for Chase. I try Chase's number; his phone rings out. Damn it. What's with these two and not answering their phones? Theo and

Matteo wouldn't actually kill Ash's best friend, would they? I have to believe they wouldn't.

"I'm going to take a bath," I say, walking out of the room, only to have Romeo and Luca follow me. I spin around on them. "Are you planning on joining me in the tub?" I glare.

"Ah, no. Gross, Lil." Romeo scrunches his face up like he ate something sour.

"We'll just sit at the door. Come on, princess, don't make this harder on us," Luca adds.

"Fine. Be my guest. Sit at the door. See if I care." I storm up to my bedroom and slam the bathroom door in their faces. I run the bath and pour in some salts and bubbles, before I open the door again and peek my head out. "Don't go through my shit. And one of you needs to get me a bottle of wine and a glass." I shut the door.

"Not your servants, Lil. Get your own wine," Romeo's muffled voice calls back.

Opening the door again, I arch an eyebrow. "Really. Fine. It's been a few days since I called Uncle T. Maybe I should give him another ring. Catch him up on all the shit you two have been getting into this past week."

They look at each other; they know I'm not bluffing. "Fine, I'll get the fucking wine, your highness," Luca grumbles as he stomps out of the room.

Romeo stares at me. "What?" I ask.

"You're more ruthless than I ever gave you credit

for, coz. Maybe you'll actually survive this world you've married yourself into."

"I married Alex, not his job," I say defensively.

"You always marry the job when you marry someone like Alessandro." Romeo squints his eyes at me. "Why aren't you worried about Hope anymore? What do you know that I don't?"

"Nothing. Of course I'm worried about my sister. How dare you try to say otherwise." I go to slam the door on his face, but he sticks his booted foot out to stop it.

"Nope, you're a bad fucking actress, Lil. What's going on?"

"I don't know what you're talking about." Then I smile. I know there are at least a dozen men lurking around these walls. "You know, all I'd have to do is scream, and I could have you dragged out of here."

Romeo laughs, like full-on laughs. "Harsh, Lil. But try it. You really think any of the goons your husband has on his payroll are a match for Luca and me?"

"Probably not, but I'm willing to give it a go."

"If you were, you would have done it by now."

Luca walks back in with a bottle of red and a glass. "Impressive collection you've got yourself, Lil," he says, handing the items over.

"Thanks. Now, if you'll excuse me, I have some drinking and bathing to do." I shut and lock the door.

Pouring myself a glass of wine, I sink into the tub. It's more of an indoor jacuzzi, really. This thing is bloody huge and has jets all the way around it. As grateful as I am that Hope is okay, I think I might actually kill her myself for making me worry like that. Someone wanted Alex to panic, to think I was taken. *But who?* I wonder if Alex knows who sent the text, or blew up his beach house. Someone is obviously after him, and that thought sends a chill down my spine. I can't lose him when I've only just got him.

My phone rings from the counter. I contemplate ignoring it, but I decide to stand and answer the call. I'm glad I did because it's Alex.

"Is everything okay?" I rush out, sinking back down into the water.

"Yeah, everything's good, babe. Josh is driving Hope to our place now. We're all on our way home. She was fine. According to her, her phone died, and she got *side-tracked* with Chase." Alex emphasizes the word *side-tracked.*

"Is Chase okay?" I ask, fearing what fate my cousins have for him. Chase isn't like Alex; he's not going to stand up to the freaking mafia like a madman.

"Define okay?"

"Alex, Chase is one of our very good friends. Is he still breathing?"

"Yes."

"Is he bleeding?"

"A little." His answers are vague and short on purpose. I know Alex won't lie to me, but that doesn't mean he'll be all that forthcoming with information either. I have to be smart and ask the right questions around him if I want to know shit.

"What happened?"

"I'll fill you in when we get home. Don't worry, he'll survive. As much as Theo wanted to kill him, he didn't. We'll be there in ten."

"Okay, I love…" The sound of gunfire in the next room halts my sentence. I freeze. Fuck, my cousins are in that room. I can hear shouting over the firefight.

"Lily! What the hell is going on?" Alex's voice yells through the receiver.

"Alex, please tell me you have a gun hidden in the bathroom somewhere?" I whisper.

"Lily, what's happening?" He's panicked. The engine of his car roars and his tyres spin.

"Guns, Alex, where are they?" I whisper again. I will not die naked in the bloody bath. I don't know who the hell is in the house. I can still hear Romeo and Luca yelling and cursing, all of which is in Italian, and I have no idea what they're saying. Why didn't I ever learn to speak the bloody language? Uncle T tried to get me to take lessons for years. My excuse was I'd never need to know it, because if I ever went to Italy, I'd just drag one of the boys around with me to translate.

"What bathroom are you in?" Alex asks.

"Our bedroom."

"Okay, third drawer on the right. I want you to lock the door, Lil. Do not step out of that bathroom. Let your cousins handle it. They have it under control. Just stay in the bathroom. If anyone gets through the door, shoot."

"Okay." My fingers tremble as I wrap a towel around me. I'd like to have faith that my cousins have this under control, but if they do, why the hell can I still hear gunshots?

26

"What the hell! Get out!" Hope yells, scrambling for the sheet to cover herself.

"Hope, get dressed. We're leaving." I pick up a discarded shirt from the floor and throw it at her.

"Ah, no, *you're* leaving." She pulls the shirt over her head.

"Look, I think maybe you all should put the guns down," Chase says in an eerily calm voice.

"Yeah, you see, I would. But that there is my cousin you're bangin'. So, sorry, not gonna happen," Theo growls.

"Theo, no. You don't get to come into town and act like you're the boss of me. You're not even *the boss.* Maybe I should call Uncle T." Hope gets out of the bed. I tuck my gun into my waistband, ready to pick her ass up and drag her home.

"Hope, do you have any idea what you've put your sister through tonight?" I ask, attempting to rein in my anger.

"What do you mean? Where is Lily?"

"She's at home, which is exactly where we are going. Get your shit." I walk towards the door and wait.

"If you think I'm leaving Chase here with these three psychopaths, then you're just as nuts as they are. I'm not leaving." She picks up her phone.

"I just had to hold my fucking wife while she fell apart, because she thought the worst had happened to you. I don't care if I have to carry you out of here myself, you are coming. Lily needs to see that you're okay. *With her own two eyes,*" I growl, stepping towards her.

"Fine, I'll go to your place. Josh will drive me. And Theo and Matteo will ride with us." She looks at me and smiles. "Just what, exactly, do you think Lily will do when she finds out you're the reason her sister's heart is broken beyond repair?"

"What the fuck are you talking about?" I look to her cousins for any indication they understand her. They seem just as confused.

"If anything happens to him, I'll die of a broken heart. I won't survive that. How do you think Lily will feel if that happens?"

Fuck, she's striking low with that one. So, I do the only thing I can do. The only thing that will probably save Chase's ass from the Valentino brothers. I call Ash.

"Yeah," he groans as he answers. I guess he's still pissed about the whole taking Breanna to get Faith back without him knowing thing.

"The Valentinos are about to pop a cap in your boy Chase. You might want to get to his place if you want to stop them." I hear the sharp intake of his breath.

"What the fuck's going on? Why are they goin' after him?"

"Long story, but we thought Hope was abducted, Josh tracked her to your boy's house, and the Valentino brothers just walked in on him screwing their cousin."

"Fuck!" Chase curses under his breath and shakes his head.

"Fuck!" Ash screams the same sentiment. I hear glass smashing in the background, right before the phone cuts out.

"Really? I didn't take you for a rat, Alex," Hope seethes.

I shrug my shoulders. "I don't have time for this shit. Are you bringing her to mine, or do I need to drag her out kicking and screaming?" I ask Josh.

"I'll drop her off at yours," he agrees.

"Fine. Try not to kill him." I point to Chase. "I'm sure Ash is going to want words with him first." I leave them all behind. I need to get home to Lily. Obviously, Hope is fine.

We're halfway through the drive home when I turn to Leo. "Whoever sent that picture wanted me to think they had Lily. What the fuck is their game?" As soon as the words are out of my mouth, it hits me. *It's a distraction.* They're drawing me away. Dread fills the pit of my stomach. I call Lily. I need to hear her voice.

As we're about to hang up, I hear the unmistakable sound of gunshots in the background, and Lily's panicked voice is asking where the guns are hidden. I direct her to where she'll find not one, but two loaded weapons, however the knowledge gives me no peace of mind.

"Fucking go faster, Leo." Fuck, Lily isn't the only one in that house. Mia and Tessie are there too. I don't want to hang up on Lily. I can't hang up. "Give me your phone." Leo points to the centre console. "Lily, I'm going to call Mia on Leo's phone. Stay on this line. Do not hang up. I'll be back in a sec."

"Okay," she whispers.

I scroll through Leo's phone until I find Mia's

number. She answers on the first ring. "Leo, where's Alex?"

"It's me. Are you with Tessie? You need to get yourselves into a safe room now."

"We're fine, Alex. Tessie and I are in the safe room in her bedroom. I brought her straight in as soon as I heard the shots. What's happening?" she asks.

"Turn the screens on. They're hooked up to the cameras." I wait while she flips the switches.

"Okay. But where's Lily? I can't see her, Alex."

"She's in the master bath. How many, Mia? How many men are in the house?"

"Oh shit, there're only two that I can see. They're in the hall, outside your bedroom."

"Okay, good. Where the fuck are all the guards?" I ask out loud.

"I-I don't see any."

"Mia, stay in the safe room. Don't come out until Leo or I get you." I hang up, knowing my sister will stay put. She won't risk Tessie for anything. Holding my own phone against my ear, I grit out, "Lily, are you still there, babe?"

"Ah, yeah, what's going on, Alex?"

"There are two men outside the bedroom door. Your cousins are holding them off by the sounds of it. I just need you to stay put, Lily. Do not leave the bathroom. I'll be there real soon."

"Okay. Do you want kids?" Her question has me smiling. *Odd time to be discussing the future.*

"With you, yes. I want a football team."

"I'm not pushing a football team out my vagina, Alex. Maybe we could adopt?" she suggests.

"Maybe. How about you? How many do you want?"

"Ah, four. I always envied my cousins for having more than one sibling. They're all so close, but maybe that's just a mafia family thing, you know. I mean, Hope and I are as close as you can get, but we're twins. It's different when you're twins. I think... I don't know."

Her ramblings soothe the ache that settled in my heart... a little. It's weirdly comforting. I need to keep her talking. "What will our four children's names be?"

"Um, I don't know. I've never really thought about it," she whispers. I hear a bang, then loud cursing in the background. "Shit, Alex, I love you, like really, really love you. More than I've ever loved anything in my life. I love you more than I love the ocean. I really freaking love the ocean." The line goes dead.

"Lily?" I check the screen, knowing she's hung up. I redial her number, but it goes straight to voicemail. "Fuck, Leo, get me to the fucking house *now*!" I yell.

He looks over at me but doesn't say a word. He does, however, put his foot down harder on the accelerator. Two minutes later, we're flying up the drive of my estate. The gates were wide open, no guards in sight. Leo pulls right up to the front door. I don't wait. I take off running through the house, heading for my bedroom. I momentarily pause in the foyer, seeing

Gary, one of my long-time guards, bleeding out on the floor. *Fucking hell.*

Taking two steps at a time, I stop at the threshold of the master bedroom. One guy is on the floor in the hallway, just outside the door, a bullet between his eyes. The other is standing inside the room, a gun held right to Lily's head. I stop dead in my tracks.

"Right on time, Alex. You'll get to see me break your little whore wife here." Lily's oddly calm. She's looking straight at me. I'm losing my mind. What the fuck do I do? Romeo's got a gun pointed at Bandetto—the fucker won't get out of here alive. He knows that, which means he's got nothing to lose.

Luca is on the ground, clutching his stomach with one hand and shakily holding a gun up with the other. How the fuck did they let him get this close to Lily? There are a million questions running through my head right now. But the most important one is: *how the fuck do I get Lily out of harm's way, so I can fucking skin this fucker alive?*

27

The look in Alex's eyes is feral. I can see how much he wants to get his hands on this dickhead who currently has a gun to my head. How the hell did I get into this situation? *I'm an idiot, that's how.* I should have stayed in the bathroom like Alex asked me to—no, he begged me to stay locked away.

I heard Luca's scream of pain and ran right out into the arms of a crazed man. What the hell was I thinking? I'm officially that stupid girl in all the horror films, the one who runs up the stairs, thinking she can get away from the axe murderer. Well, this is not going to be the end of *my* story. I'm getting my happily ever after with Alex. I just need to get myself out of this idiot's hold first. I could flip him. He's smaller than Alex, and I managed to flip him easily enough. But can I do it without getting my head blown off? *Maybe.*

I look directly at Alex and smile. "Don't worry, Alex, I'm not so easily broken. Remember Christmas Eve, when Hope tried to take me down?" I'm hoping that's enough of a hint for him to know what I'm about to do. It'd probably be better if I was freaking wearing clothes, instead of just a towel—albeit the fluffiest, softest towel I've ever used. I need to find out where Alex gets these from. My mum would go nuts for them.

"Lily, no." Alex grits his teeth. I can see a look of sheer terror on his face, which gives me all the more courage to do whatever I can to get out of this situation.

"Yes," I say, as my foot stomps down and my head goes back, ramming the jerk in the nose. Then I bend and pull. Somehow, in all of the chaos, I don't end up with a bullet in my head. Instead, I'm standing over top of him, drawing the gun I've been hiding under the towel. "You know, people always underestimate me. I don't know why." I smirk.

He doesn't get to answer before Alex pulls the trigger, putting a bullet directly between his eyes. I look up to Alex, then back down at the guy with a hole in his head. Holy shit, I know I can talk a tough game and all, but I've never actually seen a dead body. I've never seen someone killed before. Alex just shot him, no hesitation, just pulled the trigger. Like it was second nature for him to end a life.

I should feel something other than sheer relief, right? I should feel... something. I sink down to the ground. There's a lot of commotion around us. A lot of people have entered the room, but it's all white noise. Alex curses before he bends down and picks me up, carrying me out. He goes into Tessie's room and presses a button on the wall. The bookshelf full of ornaments slides across, opening to another room.

"What the hell happened, Alex?" Mia questions.

"I'll fill you in later. It's safe now, but take Tessie down to the theatre or something. Keep her away from this level for a while." Alex doesn't wait for a response. He turns on his heel and walks out, with me still in his arms.

My fingers are curled around his shirt. If he thinks he's ever getting out of my sight again, he's going to see just how crazy I can get. I close my eyes and drown in everything that is Alex. His scent. The hardness of his chest. The heat of his skin as I undo a few of his buttons, sliding my hand under the fabric of his shirt.

Alex lowers me down onto a bed. I look around. How many rooms does this house have? I haven't seen this one before. It's decorated in gold and white fabrics, which drape from the bed and curtains. There's a gold velvet sofa off to the side, with a lamp table next to it.

"Why the fuck didn't you stay in the fucking bathroom, Lily?" Alex grits out between his clenched teeth. I watch him stand and pace the short length of the room.

Whoa, hold up! He's mad at me? "What the hell are you mad at me for? I'm not the one who has crazy assholes breaking into the house, looking to rape and torture me. That shit is all on you, Alex. That guy was out to hurt you, and he had no problem using me to do it."

His face pales. Slumping down into the chair, he lowers his head, grabbing at his hair with both hands. "Fuck. You're right. This is my fault. You could have been killed because of me. I never should have brought you here."

"What?" My palms start to sweat. He's not doing this to me. He can't do this to me.

"Lily, you shouldn't be mixed up in my shit. I knew you were too good for me, but I was a selfish bastard and took you anyway. I can't stomach the thought of something else happening to you. I need to let you go." His mouth might be saying the words, but his eyes argue otherwise.

It's the fear talking. He thinks he's doing what he *should* do. I need to make him see that he's an idiot for even suggesting he can let me go. "You can't handle the thought of me being hurt? But you can handle the thought of me hooking up with other men? You want to let me go and live out my life, with someone who isn't you? Have someone else's children?" The feral growl he emits lets me know I've hit my mark. "You probably should have thought of that before you put a fucking ring on it, Alex. News flash, we're married. You can't just get rid of me that easily. You can try, you can push me away, but I'm not going anywhere." I'm full-on yelling at him now; tears run freely down my face.

"Fuck, Lily! You think I want this? You think I want to let you go? I can't fucking get through five minutes without thinking about you. Picturing you with someone else makes me want to eradicate every other fucking male on this planet. But seeing you with a gun held to your fucking head? I've never been more scared of anything in my fucking life, Lily."

I stand and walk over to him. Forcing his body to lean back in the chair, I straddle his lap. "I'm not going anywhere. I need you, Alex. I need you more than I've ever needed anything."

His hands snake up under my towel, and his palms squeeze the globes of my ass. "Fucking hell, Lily, how is it—even at a time like this—all I can think about is driving my cock into that sweet-ass pussy of yours?"

"Do it," I challenge. I unwrap the towel from my body and drop it to the floor. There's something erotic about being naked on top of him while he's still fully clothed.

"Fuck, you're perfect." Alex's mouth goes to my

breast, his tongue flicking my hardened nipple. One of his hands travels down between our bodies. Without warning, he shoves two fingers into me. They slide in easily. I'm so wet already.

"Oh God, I need you." I fumble with his belt buckle; he removes his fingers to help me. As soon as we've managed to free his cock, I have it lined up with my entrance. I sink down onto him. "Fuck. Alex, I need you to fuck me now."

He grips my hips so tightly I'm sure I'll be sporting bruises for the next few days. "With pleasure." He guides my hips up and down his shaft. Hard. Fast. *Relentlessly.* Each thrust sends me closer and closer to the edge of bliss, until we're both soaring. With our hearts beating erratically, Alex lays me down on the bed. His arms band around me like he's afraid to let me go.

"Alex?"

"Yeah?"

"Next Christmas, let's go somewhere it snows. Like Canada or Europe."

He lets out a strangled laugh. "I'll book the flights now. How do you think your family will cope if you're not there for Christmas?"

Now it's my turn to laugh. "They will hunt us down and follow us. They're a little nuts over the holiday season."

EPILOGUE

Lily

Twelve months later

I can't believe he was able to do this. Not only did Alex deliver on a white Christmas, but he somehow managed to find a place large enough for everyone—which is no small task, considering how bloody big my extended family is.

We've come a long way in the last year, but the biggest change is what I'm looking at now. Alex and Theo, sitting in the living room, each nursing a whiskey glass while deep in conversation. They've developed some kind of weird-as-hell bromance, constantly exchanging phone calls and text messages. Alex tries to blow it off as just business, but you don't have heart-to-hearts about personal issues with your "just business" associates. I'm pretending to be engrossed in my book, but really, my ears are honed in on their conversation. Apparently, there's a woman back in New York who doesn't throw herself at Theo's feet. Go figure! I didn't know such creatures existed. *Cue eyeroll here.*

I pull my phone out and text Hope, even though she's in this house somewhere. I'm not prepared to move, in case I miss out on some more juicy goss. These two men gossip more than anyone I know.

Me: There's a woman in New York who won't fall in line at Theo's command!! He's torn up over it.

Hope: Wait, there's someone who doesn't want Theo? What kooky world have we entered?

Me: I know, right? I need a name. Ask Romeo. He's the easiest to break.

Hope: On it. Give me five.

I smile. I know it won't be long before I can bust Theo's balls over this woman. He deserves it for how he tried to scare Alex away when we first met. Actually,

I think he had every intention of killing him and hiding the body. But *scare away* sounds less... intense.

Not even two minutes later, Hope comes through for me.

Hope: Name's Maddie. She works in a coffee shop. Theo goes in there twice a day.

Me: Perfect. Thanks.

"Hey, Theo, how's the coffee in New York?" His head spins around, his icy glare directed at me.

"Why?"

I shrug. "Just wondering if Maddie's coffee was better than the crap I had to endure last time I was there?" I use my most innocent voice.

"I'm gonna fucking kill him." Theo storms from the room, yelling out to Romeo as he goes.

I laugh. "Really, Lily? The guy's torn up over this girl. You shouldn't tease him," Alex scolds me.

"Alex, you're either Team Lily or Team Theo. Choose your side wisely," I warn him.

"I'll always be Team Lily." He picks me up and sits in my spot, with me now straddling his lap.

"Good choice, because I don't lose. Besides, it's fun —uncharted waters—to have someone who can resist one of my cousins."

"That's weird, even for your family." Alex laughs.

Speaking of family, this is the moment my dad and uncles decide to enter the room. "Lily, no. Just no," my dad grunts.

"Jesus, you must have a bloody death wish," Zac mumbles to Alex, who smirks.

"Bray, cover your ears," Alex says. My dad shakes his head in response, and leaves the room. Alex then looks directly at each of my uncles with a smile. "You do know we're married, don't you? We do all the things married people do. Only, we do them better, don't we, babe?"

I can feel my face heat up, the blush creeping along my neck. "Oh, we do them so much better. Actually, Alex, I need you to help me with something in the bedroom—*now*." I stand and spin around to the four stony faces of my uncles.

"Lil Pill, take it back. Please," Uncle Zac pleads.

"Fuck it. No one will ever find the body. Let me at him," Uncle T says.

"I'll help." Josh shares a look with Uncle T.

"And that's our cue to leave, while we still can." I grab Alex's hand and run out of the room. "Seriously, Alex, what the hell? I'm starting to think you *do* have a bloody death wish."

"Nope, but I sure do love seeing the pained expressions on their faces."

I lean up and whisper in his ear, "I really do need you to take me to the bedroom and fuck me now, Alex." I don't get to finish the sentence before I find myself thrown over his shoulder.

Christmas morning is utter chaos. But I wouldn't have it any other way. Bray is in his element, screaming at everyone to hurry up and gather around the tree, or should I say *trees.* Yep, there are three fucking Christmas trees, all full to the brim with gifts.

How the fuck do they think they're getting all of this shit home? *Not my problem.*

"Alex, I have a gift for you, but I... um... I need you to come open it now. In our room." Lily looks nervous; her eyes are darting around.

Leaning in, I whisper in her ear, "Lily, if the gift is

your pussy, now's probably not the best time. As much as it pains me to say that."

"No, it's not. But now that you mention it, it could be." She raises her eyebrows suggestively. *Damn this woman!* She just has to be in the same room as me, and my cock is standing at attention. I cannot get enough of her.

"Let's go." I take her wrist and lead her out, leaving the chaos of our family behind us. Lily's hands shake as she offers me a small box. "Why are you nervous? Is it a bomb?" I joke.

"Of sorts." She shrugs.

I can't take the suspense. I lift the lid and look down at the stick that's placed on top of white tissue paper. For a moment, I'm speechless. Then it hits me. *Holy fucking hell.*

"Is this...? Are you...? Are we...?" I can't even get the words out; the smile that forms on my face is foreign. I've never felt anything like this before.

"It is, I am, and we are. We're pregnant," Lily confirms. I'm stunned. We haven't been trying, but we sure as fuck haven't been careful either. "Alex, say something? Are you mad?"

"Mad? No, babe, not mad. A little shocked, and a lot fucking ecstatic. You're knocked up with my kid. Holy shit, Lily. We're having a baby."

"Shhh, keep your voice down. I don't want everyone knowing yet. It's early."

"How early?" I ask, looking at her still very flat

stomach.

"Around seven weeks."

"This is the best fucking Christmas gift I've ever received." I throw the box on the bed and pick her up, slamming my lips down on hers.

She pulls away. "As much as I want to stay in here and have you unwrap *me*, we need to get back out there before my dad comes looking for us."

"You're right. Let's go. Wait, are you okay? Do you need anything? Should I get a doctor out here or something?"

"What? *No.* I'm fine, Alex. It's not like I'm the first woman on earth to be pregnant." She laughs.

"Yeah, but you're the first woman to be pregnant *by me.*"

"And the bloody last, Alex," she growls. I think I'm going to have a lot of fun with a pregnant Lily.

As soon as we enter the living room again, everyone stops and stares at us.

"Where've you two been? Actually, don't answer that," Bray says.

"Lily's pregnant," I blurt out. Gasps and squeals fill the silence.

"Great way to keep it quiet, Alex." She elbows me in the ribs.

"Sorry, babe, but this is the most exciting thing that's ever happened to me. Besides marrying you."

I can't believe this is my life now. I have everything I never fucking knew I needed.

Are you dying to find out the story of how Uncle T came to be Uncle T?
Read all about Holly and T's story in the Valentino Empire Trilogy.

*H*ere's a little snippet from their beginning.

DEVILISH KING

*H*olly

The incessant ringing breaks through my sleep-fogged brain. I reach out an arm, trying to swipe my phone off the bedside table, only to swipe through air. I bolt upright, scanning my surroundings. It's dark, with the only glow of light coming from the doorway and the floor, where my phone is lying in wait.

The ringing stops only to start back up again straight away. I breathe a sigh of relief once recognition settles in. It's okay. I'm in my own apartment. There's nothing to be afraid of here. I jump off the bed and pick up the phone, seeing that it's two a.m. I must have been really jet-lagged. I never intended to actually sleep when I went to lay down.

"Reilly, it's two in the morning. Why are you calling me?" I answer.

"Well, thank god. Bray, it's okay. She's alive!" Reilly yells out, not bothering to move her mouth away from the phone and deafening me in the process.

"I'm alive. *Obviously.* I was asleep."

"I've been trying to call you for the last two hours, Holly. I had Bray booking flights to New York, so I could come and hunt down your murderer and avenge your death." I know she's joking, at least I hope she is. I don't laugh though; the whole *avenging death* isn't a laughing matter in our family. That's exactly how my dad ended up behind bars. "Shit, sorry, Hol. I was kidding. Mostly," Reilly says. "So, how's The Big Apple? Huh, I just got it."

"Got what?" My brain is still too far in sleep land for her riddles.

"The Big Apple. You moving to a city called The Big Apple. It's ironic, because you're a teacher and teachers eat apples and all that."

"I haven't had nearly enough sleep or coffee to even summon up a response to that one, Rye."

"You should have called. I was worried. I don't do worried very well. I think I actually got a few grey hairs, which I'm sure if you look in the mirror, you'll have them too."

"Rye, you're a redhead. You'll be safe from grey hairs for a while yet."

"Well, I need you to call me—*every day.* Let's set a time, and if you don't check in at that time every day, then I'll book a flight to come hunt down your murderer."

"Or here's a thought. Let's not," I suggest. I have no intentions of playing into her neurotic control freak of a mind.

"Okay, I'm thinking four p.m. New York time. Call me, text, send photo evidence like the day's newspaper with your face in the picture so I know it's you."

"Rye, I gotta go. I need to find food and coffee. I came straight from the airport and crashed. I'll call you later."

"Okay, promise me you'll call later. Please, Holly." Reilly's tone is more serious; she's on the verge of tears. I can hear how hard this is for her. I have to get off the phone before I start crying, and tell her I'm coming home.

"I promise. I'm okay, Rye. And I promise I'll be careful, and I'll call you later."

"I just really love you, Holly, like as much as I love myself, and that's a freaking lot."

"I love you too, Rye. What's not to love? You're a carbon copy of me." I laugh.

"Okay, call me back later."

"I will."

I hang up the phone and look around the eerily quiet room. I should make the bed; all the bedding is in a pile at the foot of it. I'll get to it after coffee. I pull my phone out and do a Google search to see if there's any place to get coffee and food, preferably somewhere nearby and open at two a.m.

I guess it's true what they say: *New York really is the city that never sleeps.* The list of restaurants, cafés, and bars within walking distance is endless. I throw on my coat, slip my feet back into my boots, and grab my purse. Locking up, I don't consider that it's literally the middle of the night, and I'm about to walk the streets of New York. *By myself.* Until my feet hit the pavement...

There are a few people brushing past. I can do this. The sidewalks are lit up with heaps of streetlights. Looking down at my phone, I see that I just need to walk a few blocks until I get to a business district. There's a twenty-four-hour café that came up on my search, so that's where I'm headed.

There's a slight chill in the air, but it's not too cold. It's just colder than what I'm used to September being. This is when it starts warming up in Sydney, easing you into the scorching summer months. But this year, I'll get that white Christmas I've always dreamed of having. I can't wait to see the snow, to experience a New York winter.

The song by Alicia Keys, "Empire State of Mind," plays on repeat in my head as I walk down the street. This is where I'll discover the new me. I'm confident that exciting things are going to happen here. I'm going to love this city. I can blend into the crowd, get lost with the herd, and not be noticed.

I can be anything—and anyone—I want to be here. Nobody knows me. Nobody knows my family's history.

They don't know my brother died.

They don't know that my dad murdered his killer and ended up behind bars.

They don't know that I'm the twin sister of Reilly Williamson, who is the wife of Bray Williamson.

They don't know me.

With this knowledge, I hold my head high. I try to smile at people as I pass by, but I get weary looks in return, as they step further aside to give me a wider berth. Okay, note to self: *tone down the smiling*. I probably look like a crazy person.

After ten minutes, I find the twenty-four-hour café. I made it here in one piece. *See? I can do this.* Pushing on the heavy door, I'm engulfed by the warmth of the fire that's blazing off to the side. It feels homey, with big soft-looking brown leather couches surrounding the mantle place. Surprisingly, no one is sitting there, although the booths are plenty full of patrons.

It's odd that this many people are out at two a.m. on a Tuesday night. I look around, thinking I'll just find a booth to sit in, but those couches... that fire... They're calling to me. Smiling at the waitress who looked up at me as I entered the store, I walk over and drop into one of the single sofas next to the fire.

And all the commotion suddenly stops. I glance up, and all at once, everyone seems to be looking away from me. Everyone except the waitress who is staring my way with wide eyes.

Great, just my luck. The first place I choose to visit in this city is getting robbed, the moment I walk into it. My strangled breaths part my lips, my heart rate picks up, and my palms sweat. This can't be happening to me.

I look around, needing to see what's going on. Except... nothing's happening. I don't see anyone holding out a gun. No one is yelling demands. People aren't scrambling to hide under tables. No, they're all just looking at me, or trying to inconspicuously look in my direction.

I peek down at my coat and wipe at my face. What the bloody hell are they all gawking at? I can feel the red creep up my neck. My hands shake a little as I fidget with my purse. I pull my phone out, deciding to focus on that. Maybe they'll all turn away once they notice I'm no one special.

I scroll through my Insta feed—although the more I scan the photos, the more homesick I feel. I hear the bell on the door, signaling someone's entrance. *Do not look up, Holly.*

I keep my eyes on my phone, like it's the most interesting thing I've ever seen. The hair on the back of my neck stands up; chills sweep over my body. This is more than just a room full of people staring at me. This reaction is different. I remind myself not to look up.

My eyes stay on my screen, even when I hear a gravelly voice say something loudly in what sounds like Italian. As much as I want to sneak a glance, to see who the owner of that voice is, I don't. I count to ten. My knee shakes as I fight my own body's response to that voice. I get to five, before I give in and raise my eyes. But all I see is the back of two men walking through a door labelled: *staff only*.

Maybe it's the owner.

When I peer around the café, everyone has gone back to eating, drinking, and whatever else they were doing before they were staring at me like I'm the new circus freak in town. Even the waitress appears as though she has recovered from whatever that was. She strolls over to me with a huge smile on her face and a notepad in her hand. I notice a slight tremor to her fingers as she grips the pen tightly.

"Good evening, what can I get for you, ma'am?" she asks politely.

"Oh, hi! Um, I haven't had a chance to look at the menu. What's good?"

"Oh my, you're Australian?" Her smile is genuine now.

"I am," I answer, unsure what else to say to that.

"I've always wanted to go to Australia. It's on my bucket list."

"Oh, you should. It's a great country," I say, picking up the menu from the coffee table in front of me.

"Oh my God, I'm so sorry! You asked what's good. But honestly, the chef will make whatever you want."

Huh, whatever I want? *Weird.* "So, if all I really wanted was some Vegemite toast, he'd be able to rustle that up for me?" I deadpan.

"Uh, I'm—sure, he'll do it. It might just take a little while. But if that's what you want, I'll pass it onto the chef." Shit, she looks nervous.

"I'm only joking. I don't want Vegemite toast. But it's interesting how far this place will go to serve the customer. Can I just have a ham and cheese toastie, and the biggest chai latte you offer?'

"Ah, sure thing." I watch her write down my order, then she looks at me again. "Ah, so a toastie is like... what, exactly?" Her eyebrows draw down in confusion.

"Oh, it's a toasted sandwich, with ham and cheese on it. You know, I can just look at the menu and order something that's normally on there."

"No, it's fine. That's what I thought, just checking that we were talking about the same thing. Your order won't be long." With that, she's gone, leaving me alone with my thoughts.

The tiny hairs on my neck prickle again. I feel like I'm being watched, but when I glance around, no one is paying me any attention. If anything, it looks like they're all desperately trying not to look my way.

My order comes out really quickly, considering how busy this place seems. Twenty minutes later, I'm ready to go back home, shower, make the bed, and sleep for another few hours.

"How was everything?" the same waitress asks when I approach the counter.

"That was probably the best toastie I've ever had." I smile, telling her the truth. If toasties could have five stars, that would have been a five-star toastie.

"Oh, I'm glad. Here, before you go, this is for you too." She hands me a small white box.

"What is it?" I ask.

"Red velvet cake."

"Oh, I didn't order this." I try to hand it back to her. But she holds her palms up, refusing to accept it.

"I know you didn't. Someone else wanted you to have it. Thank you so much for dining with us. We hope we'll see you here again soon."

"Uh, sure." I'm confused... Who would have ordered me cake? I don't know anyone here. I pull out my wallet and find a fifty, handing it over to the waitress.

"I can't take that." She looks at the money like it has the ability to burn her.

"What do you mean? How much do I owe you? I don't think I have anything smaller." Surely fifty dollars is more than enough to cover my order.

"No, I mean, you don't need to pay. Your meal was already covered." The waitress then turns around and walks out the back, leaving me more confused than ever.

I pull a pen and paper out of my bag and write down a little note. I don't know who thinks they can pay for my order, but I don't need anyone's money. I wrap the note around the fifty and leave it on the counter. Hopefully no one else takes it before the waitress returns.

The whole walk home I have that same feeling, like someone is watching me. *Following me.* Yet, every time I turn around, no one is there. It freaks me out enough to quicken my strides. I make it back to my building in five minutes, locking the door and turning on every light in the empty apartment.

I spend the next five minutes pacing the small space, before I decide to shake the feeling off as me being paranoid in a new city.

DEVILISH KING

Theo

"You know I'm trying my fucking hardest to tune you the fuck out, right, Neo? I can't do that when you're constantly yapping about this shit." I grunt at my cousin, who is also my right-hand man. Although, I could be on the hunt for a new right-hand if he doesn't shut the fuck up.

As tempted as I am to pop a cap in his ass and silence him for good, he's one of my best capos. Mafia rules say you can't shoot a made man just because you're sick of their voice. Whoever the fuck thought that one up hadn't met Neo.

There's also the fact that, despite his annoying-as-fuck personality, he's my best friend. The one person in this world I trust to have my back. *Always*. No matter how fucked up a situation is, I know he'll be by my side, guns blazing. Fuck, he's so loyal he'd willingly follow me into the pits of hell and face off with the devil himself.

"Yeah, well, someone has to talk some fucking sense into that thick skull of yours. You're seriously going to tie yourself to her, to that family? For what? Because your papa says so? Fuck that. It ain't the fucking fifteenth century, man. Arranged marriages should not be a thing anymore," Neo yells, hitting the steering wheel with his open palm.

Why is he so fucking worked up over this? It's not like he's the one getting hitched to someone he's not even remotely attracted to. Don't get me wrong. Lana, my *fiancée*, is a knockout. Beautiful. *Model-worthy even.* The problem is... I've been friends with her since we were in diapers, and she's like my fucking sister.

Why the fuck our fathers put this plan together, I have no idea. But my old man's the Don, and you don't say no to the fucking Don and live to tell the story. So, like the dutiful son I am, the underboss, I set the example and follow my father's lead. *In everything.*

Besides, it could be worse. It could always be worse. At least that's what I tell myself. "My *papa* is the fucking Don. So, yes, I am going to listen to him. Take the orders and follow through on this sham of a fucking marriage. Don't even try to tell me that you would say no to him."

"Of course I wouldn't. Believe it or not, I don't have a fucking death wish," he grumbles.

"Yeah, news flash, asshole. *Neither do I.* I just wish I knew what the fuck they're trying to achieve, by bringing the families together like this."

I don't understand why my father made this deal. Every time I've brought it up, he's shut me down with the usual nonsense of telling me it's time I settled down and started a family. I need an heir. *That kind of bullshit.* I'm fucking twenty-five years old. Why the fuck does he think I need an heir already? Maybe he's dying. If that's the case, I wish he'd do it before the nuptials. That way, I can kill the deal with Lana's father myself.

It's not that I don't love my father. *I do.* I even respect the hell out of him. He's always been someone I've looked up to, someone I've thrived to be like. My father rules with an iron fist, a bloody one at that. But he's not just feared; he's respected among the men. I only hope I can be half the boss he is when it's my turn to lead the family.

Neo pulls up to the shopfront. "You ready to have some fun?" he asks with a smile.

The bastard is bloodthirsty crazy. This is the part of the job I do because I have to. But Neo? He does it 'cause he fucking likes it. I think he gets off on the violence.

"As I'll ever be. Let's get this over with. I'm craving your sister's lasagna."

Neo laughs. "I should tell Aunt Gloria that you like Helena's lasagna better than hers." He jumps out of the car, dodging the punch I was throwing his way.

"She would never believe you anyway." I smirk. My mother thinks I'm Noble Prize worthy; she's my biggest fucking cheerleader. I'm sure if you asked her, she'd tell you the sun shone right out of my ass. But she's Italian—most of the women are like that with their sons.

"I've got photo evidence of you eating at Helena's. A lot of it," he continues as we walk into the storefront. The little bell hanging on the door informs the occupants of our arrival.

It doesn't matter though. There's nowhere they can run. *We'd find them.* If they're smart, they'll stay put and face us. If they're stupid, which they usually fucking are, they'll run and force me to chase them. I don't fucking like playing cat and mouse—it never ends well for the rodent. Thankfully, these idiots seem to be the former. They stand there, with their mouths gaping open like fucking fish out of water. If they don't pay up tonight, they might just be the fish *in* the water. With a brand-new pair of fucking cement shoes, courtesy of my father's men.

"Tsk, tsk, tsk. Neo, you know, I thought Luca and Paul here would have known better than to try and rip me off."

"Please, T, I didn't. I'll get you the money. We just need more time," Paul stutters out.

"You see, Paul, if I give you more time, then I gotta give Jo Blow down the street more time. And then his cousin. And his fucking uncle. I'd never get paid. You can see how that'd be a problem for me, right?" I say as I fold up the sleeves of my white dress shirt.

"Please, we'll get you the money. I swear." Luca tries to plead their case this time.

"Mmm, I don't know, T. They seem genuine. Maybe we should give them a chance," Neo offers. He's a fucking psychopath, letting them think he's on their side right before he strikes. I see the flash of relief cross over their eyes. It doesn't last long. Neo pulls his gun from his holster and shoots Paul's knee out. The fucker falls to the ground screaming. Meanwhile, his brother Luca just stands there with his hands in the air. "Or maybe not. We're not known to be lenient, and I wouldn't want to wreck the Valentino family name." Neo smiles.

"You're right. We're not known to be lenient. Why start now? We'll be back, same time tomorrow. Have my money for me, or it'll be more than his knee that gets blown off. You got me?" I look to the trembling man.

"Y-yes, T. I'll have it." His whole body shakes from fear. I often wonder, at this point, if I should feel empathy for these assholes. But then I remember they borrowed money from the fucking mafia. If you didn't want to end up in this situation, then go to a damn bank to get a loan.

"See to it that you do. I don't like wasting my time." With that final message, I exit the shop, Neo following right behind me.

Thank God that's over. I'm fucking starving. "Let's go. I need to eat."

"Glad a bit of blood didn't make you lose your appetite."

"Shut up. It was one fucking time." I was also fucking fourteen. Any kid that age would throw up if they watched their father skin a man alive.

"One time too many, coz."

Stepping into Helena's café, I can tell straight away something is off. I'm instantly put on high alert, and my pulse races. *What the fuck is going on?* Everyone knows this place is owned by Neo's sister. Nobody would be stupid enough to mess with it.

I scan the interior; everyone's quiet. As their eyes dart across the room, the fear is instantly recognizable, but they also look like they're waiting for something. Like they're... curious. Then I spot the object of their curiosity.

A red-haired fucking angel. That's the only way I can describe the woman currently sitting in my fucking chair. The same chair that no one dares occupy, because they know it's reserved for me. It's the best spot in the café. Right near the fireplace, yet it's also positioned to give you a view of the whole room.

My steps falter. I'm completely captivated by her. Then I remember all these people are waiting on me, waiting to see what I'll do when someone dares to sit in my chair. She's new. I've never seen her around here before. I'd remember if I had.

She's got her head buried in her phone, oblivious to the fact that all eyes are currently on her. I can see her lips are pursed, so maybe she's not that oblivious. But I can't see her eyes. I really want to see her fucking eyes.

"Torna a fare quello che stavi facendo. Chiunque tocchi quella ragazza, se la dovrà vedere con me." *Go back to what you were doing. Anyone who touches that girl will answer to me*, I tell them in my native Italian. Even if they don't understand me, I think they all get the message when I turn my back and the chatter resumes. "We'll eat out the back tonight. Make sure she gets whatever she wants, Helena." I don't wait for her reply. I know my cousin will do what I say. I walk through to the kitchen without a second glance towards the woman. As much as my whole body is aching to turn around, I don't.

Instead, I walk out back, because I know once I get

to the office, I'll have a view of the whole café. Neo made sure there's a state-of-the-art CCTV system in this place. I power on the wall of screens as soon as I get into the office, and sit on the lounge chair that faces them.

I can't believe I'm about to say this. "Maybe you're right." I glance up at Neo, who hasn't said a word since we arrived.

"I usually am. But what, exactly, am I right about this time."

"I need to get out of this fucking marriage."

"And a cute little redhead you just left sitting in your spot—a spot you won't even let me sit in, *mind you* —has nothing to do with this change of heart, right?" he prompts.

"Or everything to do with it," I say absently as I watch her interact with Helena on the screen. The thing my cousin loves the most about the café business is the customers. She refuses to leave the floor, even though she makes more than enough to hire staff to wait the tables.

Half an hour later, I watch as the red-headed vixen stands up and heads for the counter. I rise to my feet, ready to follow her wherever she's going. I need to know where this woman lives. I need to know her name. *I need to know everything.*

I smile when I watch her leave a note on the counter after Helena refused to take her cash. Walking out, I pick up her note, pocketing it as I start making my way up the street. I keep to the shadows as I trail her steps.

She's smart though. She must sense she's being followed, because she picks up her pace. I stop across the street when she enters an apartment building. I wait. Then I see it. A light turns on, and she's at the window, looking out. It's like she's staring straight at me, but I know it's impossible for her to see me where I'm hidden.

I pull the note from my pocket, finding a fifty-dollar bill wrapped around the paper. Is she nuts? She ate a grilled cheese, and she left fifty dollars?

I don't know how much I owe you, but hopefully this covers it.
Holly

Holly. I roll her name over my tongue. I like it. I fucking love it. I stand there, waiting for her lights to turn off. Surely, she'll be heading to bed soon. Then images of her sprawled out over my own bed fill my fucking head. Fuck! I really need to find a way to get out of this engagement.

I wait for over an hour. Her lights never turn off, but she doesn't appear at the window again either.

Continue reading Holly and T's story in *Devilish King, Book 1 of the Valentino Empire trilogy.*

ALSO BY KYLIE KENT

The Merge Series

Merged With Him (Zac & Alyssa's Story)

Fused With Him (Bray & Reilly's Story)

Entwined With Him (Dean & Ella's Story)

Ignited By Him (Ash & Breanna's Story)

An Entangled Christmas (Alex & Lily's Story)

McKinley
Ranch Duet

Josh & Emily's Story

Ruining Her

Ruining Him

Valentino Empire Trilogy

Theo & Holly's Story

Devilish King

Unassuming Queen

United Reign

ACKNOWLEDGMENTS

First, I'd like to acknowledge you, the reader. Without you, I would not be where I am today. Your constant support and feedback (through your messages and reviews) mean the world to me. They give me the encouragement to keep at this authoring journey. I love everything about conjuring up a story and putting it into words.

My love for everything Christmas came from my nanna. She was a little Christmas nut, and it seems I have inherited her Christmas spirit. Growing up in the tropics of the northern parts of Australia, our Christmases were always sun-filled and hot. Many hours were spent at the beach or in the backyard pool. There was always more food than anyone could possibly eat and lots of presents under the tree. My nan did not do Christmas by halves. I remember spending the Christmas weeks running around the beach with my million cousins and my sisters. And just like Lily, I do have a favourite cousin. But I'll never admit who he is, although I'm sure he knows!! I will always treasure those Christmas memories and be forever grateful to my nan for giving us such wonderful Christmas days.

I would not be able to do this without the support of my husband. Nate is my happily ever after, my forever person. The one who supports me unconditionally like no one else ever has.

My beta readers are bloody amazing women. Natasha, Amy, and Sam: You girls keep me on my toes, keep me reaching and meeting my deadlines. And make sure I'm not killing off the most important characters! I can't even imagine doing this without you girls.

My editor, Kat: She's the bloody bomb! I always have a slight panic attack when I have to send off a manuscript to her, yet she never gets frustrated or annoyed with my constant need for reassurance. My stories wouldn't be half as good without you, Kat.

ABOUT KYLIE KENT

Kylie made the leap from kindergarten teacher to romance author, living out her dream to deliver sexy, always and forever romances. She loves a happily ever after story with tons of built-in steam.

She currently resides in Perth, Australia and when she is not dreaming up the latest romance, she can be found spending time with her three children and her husband of twenty years, her very own real-life instant-love.

Kylie loves to hear from her readers; you can reach her at: author.kylie.kent@gmail.com

Visit Kylie's website and sign up for her newsletter at: www.kyliekent.com

Printed in Great Britain
by Amazon

48111041R00170